P9-BVM-963

DATE DUE

AUG 4 75	FEB 1 2 '99			
NOV 1 9 1976	APR 0 9 '09			
AUG 2 7 1977				
APR 4 1978				
DEC 2 0 '83				
JUN 1 4 '88				
MAR 2 4 '92				
MAR 2 3 '00				

JOSTEN'S NO. 30 507   ATLANTA, GA. 30336

Georges Simenon

MAIGRET AND THE LONER

TRANSLATED FROM
THE FRENCH BY
EILEEN ELLENBOGEN

A HELEN AND KURT WOLFF BOOK

HARCOURT BRACE JOVANOVICH

NEW YORK AND LONDON

Printed in the United States of America

Library of Congress Cataloging in Publication Data

Simenon, Georges, 1903–
    Maigret and the loner.
    "A Helen and Kurt Wolff book."
    Translation of Maigret et l'homme tout seul.
    I. Title.
PZ3.S5892Maegq3 [PQ2637.I53]   843′.9′12   74–23862
ISBN 0–15–155144–8

First edition
B C D E

MAIGRET AND THE LONER

1 2 3 4

5678

IT WAS ONLY NINE O'CLOCK IN THE MORNING, BUT IT
was getting very warm already. Maigret, who had taken off
his jacket, was indolently opening his mail, pausing from
time to time to glance out of the window at the motionless
leaves on the trees at the Quai des Orfèvres, and at the Seine,
which was flat and smooth as silk.

It was August. Lucas and Lapointe, along with over half
the other inspectors, were on holiday. Janvier and Torrence
had taken their holidays in July, and Maigret himself was
planning to spend most of September at his house, which
looked like an old rectory, in Meung-sur-Loire.

Every day toward early evening, for almost a week now,
a brief but violent storm, accompanied by lashing rain, had
sent the people in the streets scurrying for shelter in door-
ways. These storms dissipated the intense heat of the day,
and the cooler evenings that followed were a welcome relief.

Paris was empty. Even the street noises were different,
with intervals almost of silence.

Everywhere there were brightly colored buses from many
different countries, all invariably converging on the familiar
tourist attractions, Notre-Dame, the Louvre, the Place de
la Concorde, the Etoile, the Sacré-Coeur, and, inevitably,
the Eiffel Tower.

On the streets at this time of year it was almost a shock to
hear someone speaking French.

The Director was also on holiday, so Maigret was spared

the drudgery of the daily briefing. There was little correspondence and not much crime, other than the occasional robbery with assault.

The ringing of the telephone roused the Chief Superintendent from his torpor. He lifted the receiver.

"It's the Superintendent of the First Arrondissement. He's asking to speak to you personally. Shall I put him through?"

"Yes, I'll speak to him."

Maigret knew him well. He was somewhat affected in manner and always exquisitely turned out, but he was a genuinely cultivated man, who had been a lawyer for some years before joining the police force.

"Hello! Ascan?"

"I hope I'm not disturbing you?"

"Not in the least. I've got all the time in the world."

"I'm ringing because I've had a case dumped in my lap this morning that I thought would be just up your alley."

"What's it all about?"

"A murder . . . But it's no ordinary murder. It would take too long to explain over the telephone. When will you be free?"

"I'm free now."

"Would it be asking too much to suggest that you come over to my office? The thing is, it happened in an obscure little cul-de-sac near Les Halles."

This was 1965, and the fruit-and-vegetable market of Les Halles had not yet been transferred from Paris to Rungis.

"I'll be with you in a few minutes."

He grumbled to himself, indulging in the pretense of being inconvenienced, whereas in reality he welcomed any excuse to get away from the boring routine of the past few days. He went into the inspectors' office. Ordinarily he would have taken Janvier with him, but it was essential, in the Chief Superintendent's absence, to leave someone in charge at the Quai des Orfèvres who could be thoroughly relied upon and who was capable of acting on his own initiative.

"Come with me, Torrence. We'll take a car from the parking lot."

It was not far to the police station of the First Arrondissement, on Rue des Prouvaires. Maigret was shown straight into Superintendent Ascan's office.

"You'll be staggered when you see what I have to show you. I've never seen anything like it in all my life. I'd rather say no more for the present. Ah! Torrence . . . You'd better leave the car here. It's no distance."

They skirted Les Halles, where it was business as usual, even in August. The smell from the market, in the intense heat, was overpowering. They threaded their way through narrow little streets, hemmed in by small shops and somewhat dubious-looking rooming houses. There were vagrants loafing around here and there, one of them, a woman, so drunk that she could keep herself upright only by leaning against a wall.

"This way."

Having arrived at Rue de la Grande-Truanderie, Ascan turned into a passage so narrow that a truck would not have squeezed through.

"Here we are," he announced. "Vieux-Four Passage."

There were not more than ten old houses on either side, with a gap in the middle where a building had already been pulled down. The whole street was scheduled for demolition, and the houses had been evacuated.

Some were shored up with planks to prevent the walls from collapsing.

The Police Superintendent stopped at a house that had no glass in any of its windows. Indeed, some of the window frames had been ripped out bodily. The front door was gone, and the entrance was boarded up. Ascan removed two of the boards, which were loose, to reveal a long hallway beyond.

"Watch out for the stairs! They're very rickety, and some of the treads are missing."

There was a strong smell of dust and mildew mingled with the stench of the central market.

With all this in their nostrils, they went up two flights of stairs and came upon a boy of about twelve squatting with his back against the flaking wall. As the men came up to him, he sprang to his feet, his eyes shining.

"You're Chief Superintendent Maigret, aren't you?"

"Yes."

"Oh boy! I keep a scrapbook of newspaper clippings about you . . . all your photographs and everything . . ."

Ascan cut in to explain:

"This is young Nicolier. . . . Your first name is Jean, isn't it?"

"Yes, sir."

"His father keeps a butcher's shop on Rue Saint-Denis. It's the only one around here that stays open all through the month of August. . . . Go on, Jean, let's have your story."

"It's like I told you. . . . Most of my pals are away at the beach. Well, since there's no one to play with, I spend my time poking about the neighborhood. Even though I was born here, there are some odd corners I don't know. This morning, I spotted this house. I pulled at the boards nailed across the doorway and they came loose. So I went in and called out:

" 'Anybody at home?'

"There was no answer but the echo of my own voice. I didn't really expect there would be. I went on in, just to have a look around. You see that rickety old door over there, to the right? . . . Well, I pushed it open, and that's where I found the man. . . . I beat it as fast as I could. I was all out of breath when I got to the police station. . . .

"Do I have to go back into that room?"

"I don't think that will be necessary."

"Do you want me to wait here?"

"Yes."

The door was so rotten that it would no longer serve even as firewood. It was Maigret who pushed it open. Standing on the threshold, he could see what the Police Superintendent had meant when he had promised him a surprise.

It was a fair-sized room, and the panes of both windows had been replaced with cardboard or stiff paper. The uneven floor, with gaps of more than an inch between the boards, was covered with an incredible litter of bric-a-brac, most of it broken, all of it useless.

Dominating the room was an iron bedstead on which lay, fully dressed, on an old straw mattress, a man who was unmistakably dead. His chest was covered with clotted blood, but his face was serene.

His clothes were those of a tramp, but the face and hands suggested something very different. He was elderly, with long silvery hair shot through with bluish highlights. His eyes, too, were blue. Maigret was beginning to feel uneasy under their fixed gaze, when the Superintendent closed them.

The man had a white moustache, slightly turned up at the ends, and a short Vandyke beard, also white.

Apart from this, he was close-shaven, and Maigret saw, with renewed surprise, that his hands were carefully manicured.

"He looks like an elderly actor got up as a tramp," he murmured. "Did he have any papers on him?"

"None. No identity card, no old letters, nothing. Several of my inspectors, all assigned to this district at one time or another, came and had a look at him, but none of them recognized him, though one thought he might have seen him once or twice rummaging in trash cans."

The man was very tall and exceptionally broad-shouldered. His trousers, which had a tear over the left knee, were too short for him. His tattered jacket, fit only for the rag bag, was lying crumpled on the filthy floor.

"Has the police doctor seen him?"

"Not yet. I'm expecting him any minute. I was hoping you'd get here before anything had been touched."

"Torrence, find the nearest bistro, and ring Headquarters and ask them to tell the Forensic Laboratory to send someone along as soon as possible. They'd better let the Public Prosecutor's Department know as well."

He was still much intrigued by the face of the man on the battered iron bed. His moustache and beard were so neatly trimmed that it seemed certain he had been to a barber as recently as the previous day. As for the carefully manicured hands with their varnished fingernails, it was difficult to imagine them foraging in trash cans.

And yet the man must have been doing just that for a very long time. The whole room was crammed with the most unlikely assortment of objects, nearly all broken. An ancient coffee grinder, a number of badly chipped enamel jugs, several battered buckets with holes in them, a paraffin lamp with no wick or paraffin, a pile of odd shoes.

"I'll have to make an inventory of all this stuff."

There was a washbasin fixed to the wall, and Maigret went across and turned on the tap, with no result. As he had expected, the water had been cut off. The same went for electricity and gas. It was standard procedure with houses scheduled for demolition.

How long had the man been living here? Long enough to have collected a formidable pile of junk. There was no possibility of questioning a concierge or neighbors, since there were none. The local Superintendent went out onto the landing and spoke to the Nicolier boy.

"How about making yourself useful? Go downstairs and wait outside. Some men should be arriving in a few minutes. When they get here, show them up."

"Yes, sir."

"Don't forget to warn them about the missing treads on the stairs."

Maigret was wandering about the room, picking things up and putting them down. In the process, he came across a piece of used candle and a box of matches. The candle was stuck to the bottom of a chipped cup.

In all his professional career, he had never seen anything like this room. The more he looked, the more puzzled he became.

"How was he killed?"

"He was shot several times in the chest and stomach."

"With a large-caliber gun?"

"Medium . . . A thirty-two, most probably."

"Wasn't there anything in the pockets of his jacket?"

He could just imagine the revulsion with which the elegant and fastidious Police Superintendent had forced himself to handle those filthy rags.

"A button, some bits of string, a hunk of stale bread . . ."

"No money?"

"Just two twenty-five-centime pieces."

"And what about his trouser pockets?"

"A filthy rag, which he must have used as a handkerchief, and some cigarette butts in a cough-drop tin."

"No wallet?"

"No."

Even the vagrants from the *quais*, those who slept under the bridges, usually had papers in their pockets or, at the very least, identity cards.

Torrence, who by now had returned, was no less dumfounded than Maigret.

"They're coming right away."

Moers and his men from the Forensic Laboratory were already being led up the stairs by the Nicolier boy. They looked about them in amazement.

"Is it murder?"

"Yes . . . There's no gun in here, so there's no question of suicide."

"Where should we start?"

"With fingerprints, because we can't go very much further until he's been identified."

"He certainly looked after his hands. It seems a shame to have to mess them up."

Nevertheless, they took his fingerprints.

"Photographs?"

"Of course."

"He's fine figure of a man, isn't he? He must have been as strong as a horse."

At this point, cautious footsteps were heard mounting the stairs, followed by the appearance of the Public Prosecutor's representative, along with the Examining Magistrate, Cassure, and his clerk. All three gasped in amazement when they saw the room and its extraordinary contents.

"When was he killed?" asked the Prosecutor's representative.

"We shall soon have the answer to that. Ah! Here is Doctor Lagodinec, who should be able to tell us."

The police doctor was young, brisk, and cheerful. He shook hands with Maigret, nodded to the others, and went straight up to the bed, which stood unevenly on crooked legs, another piece of wreckage picked up in the street, no doubt, or from some vacant lot.

They all looked anxiously at the floor. With so many people in the room, it was sagging dangerously and seemed on the point of collapse.

"It wouldn't surprise me if we all fell through to the floor below," remarked the young doctor.

He waited by the bed until the photographers had completed their work and then proceeded to examine the body. He bared the chest to reveal three black holes where the bullets had penetrated.

"Three shots were fired from a distance of three feet or less. The assailant took careful aim. The spacing is very neat, as you can see, which suggests to me that the victim was asleep at the time."

"Instantaneous death, would you say?"

"Yes. One of the shots went clean through the left ventricle."

"Do you think the bullets went right through?"

"I'll tell you that when I've turned him over."

One of the two photographers helped him. There was only one exit wound in the mysterious vagrant's back. No doubt the bullet would be found lodged in the mattress.

"Is there any water in the room?"

"No. It's been cut off."

"I wonder how he managed to wash himself so thoroughly. As you can see, he kept himself very clean."

"Can you give us a rough idea of the time of death?"

"Between two and five this morning. I daresay I'll be able to narrow it down a bit after I've done the autopsy. Has he been identified?"

"Not yet. We'll have to get a picture into the papers. By the way, how soon can you let us have the first prints?"

"In about an hour. Will that do?"

The photographers departed, leaving the other technicians to get on with the job of fingerprinting everything in the room.

"I don't suppose we can be of any further use?" murmured the Public Prosecutor's representative.

"Do you want me to stay?" Judge Cassure put in.

Maigret, with an abstracted air, was slowly puffing at his pipe. It took him a second or two to realize that he was being spoken to.

"No. I'll keep you informed."

And to the police doctor:

"Was he drunk, would you say?"

"I very much doubt it, but we'll know for sure when we've examined the contents of the stomach. At first sight, at any rate, he doesn't strike me as a man who was given to drinking."

"A nondrinking vagrant?" murmured the local Superintendent. "You don't often come across such a specimen."

"Maybe he wasn't a vagrant?" Torrence suggested.

As for Maigret, he didn't say a word. His glance traveled about the room, resting here and there, as though he were making a kind of private photographic record of everything he saw, down to the smallest detail. In less than a quarter of an hour, while the technicians were still at their work, the mortuary van from the Forensic Laboratory drove into the little passage, and the Nicolier boy went downstairs to show the two stretcher-bearers the way up.

"All right, you can take him away."

One last look at the noble patriarchal head with its elegantly trimmed beard.

"The old fellow weighs a ton!" remarked one of the stretcher-bearers.

They had considerable difficulty in maneuvering their burden down the rickety stairs, with so many of the treads missing.

Maigret called out to the boy:

"Come here, son. Do you happen to know if there is a Hairdressers' School anywhere in the neighborhood?"

"Yes, Monsieur Maigret. On Rue Saint-Denis. Just three doors down from our butcher's shop."

Ten years ago or more, Maigret had visited one of these schools in search of a criminal. In some districts of Paris such places were probably quite luxuriously appointed, but one would hardly expect to find anything on a grand scale in the neighborhood of the central market.

Presumably the one on Rue Saint-Denis, like many others, relied mainly on vagrants and beggars for the inexperienced and clumsy apprentices to practice on. The apprentices usually were both male and female, some of them training as manicurists.

But there was no point in going there until he had photographs of the dead man to show. For the time being, all Maigret could do was to wait around and hope that something useful might be gleaned from the fingerprints.

He left Moers and two of his men to carry on with their work in the room, and went downstairs, accompanied by Torrence and the local Superintendent. It was a relief to breathe the relatively clean air of the cul-de-sac.

"Why was he killed, do you think?"

"I haven't the remotest idea."

Beyond the archway there was a courtyard. It was littered with old packing cases and other debris. Still, it did provide Maigret with the answer to one of the doctor's questions. Set into one of the walls was a pump, with a bucket in fairly sound condition underneath. He tried the pump. At first nothing happened, but with a little persistence he soon got the water flowing.

Here, surely, was the explanation of the unknown man's personal cleanliness. The Chief Superintendent could picture him, naked to the waist, sluicing himself down with buckets of water.

Parting company with Superintendent Ascan, he turned into the Rue de la Grande-Truanderie and in the direction of the market. It was growing hotter and hotter, and, on the pretext of having to make a telephone call, he went into the nearest fairly decent-looking bistro and ordered a glass of beer for himself and Torrence.

"Put me through to Records, will you?"

He asked for Inspector Lebel, the officer who had taken the dead man's fingerprints.

"Hello . . . Lebel? Have you had time to go through the records yet?"

"I've just come from there. There are no prints that fit those of the corpse."

Here was another anomaly. There were few vagrants who had not, at one time or another, come into conflict with the law.

"Thanks, anyway. Do you happen to know if the photographs are ready?"

"They should be in about ten minutes. . . . Ten minutes, Mestral, is that right?"

"Let's say a quarter of an hour."

They were not far from Police Headquarters, and it took the two men only a few minutes to get back to the Quai des Orfèvres. Maigret went straight up to the Photographic Section. He had to wait for the prints to dry. He had left Torrence in the inspectors' office.

A number of photographs had been taken. Armed with three copies of each, he returned to his office and instructed Inspector Loutrie to distribute them to the newspapers, especially those that had afternoon editions.

"Come along now, Torrence. We've got an hour before lunch. We'll use the time to make a few house-to-house calls."

Maigret handed Torrence a sheaf of photographs.

"Show these around in all the little shops and bars near Les Halles. I'll meet you at the car."

He himself turned to Rue Saint-Denis. It was a narrow street, crowded and noisy even at vacation time. For this little local community, seaside holidays were a rarity.

The Chief Superintendent peered at the numbers on the houses. The one he was looking for was a seed and bulb shop. To the left of the shopwindow was a passage leading into a courtyard. A flight of steps jutted out into it, next to which, fixed to the wall, were two enamel plaques that had once been green but by now had faded to an indeterminate gray.

JOSEPH
SCHOOL OF HAIRDRESSING AND MANICURE

Beneath this was an arrow pointing to the steps, and the word MEZZANINE.

Flush underneath this plaque was another, which read:

MADAME VEUVE CORDIER
ARTIFICIAL FLOWERS

Here, too, there was an arrow pointing to the steps, but this time accompanied by the words SECOND FLOOR.

Maigret mopped his brow, climbed to the mezzanine, opened a door, and found himself in a fairly large room, inadequately lighted by two narrow windows. A few naked light bulbs hanging from the ceiling did little to relieve the gloom.

There were two rows of armchairs, one for men and the other for women, it seemed. Several boys and girls were working under the direction of older men. Keeping a general eye on things was a skinny little man, almost bald, with a moustache dyed coal-black.

"You are the proprietor, I take it?"

"I am Monsieur Joseph, yes."

He could have been any age between sixty and seventy-five. Mechanically, Maigret scrutinized the men and women in the armchairs, which had undoubtedly been bought sec-

ondhand. He might have been in a Salvation Army shelter
or under the bridges, since all the men and women being
combed and clipped and shaved by the boys and girls were
vagrants. It was actually a somewhat gruesome spectacle, the
more so in that dim light. Because of the heat, the two narrow windows were open, and the street noises came in
clearly, which made the schoolroom atmosphere of the
place seem even more incongruous.

Not wishing to try Monsieur Joseph's patience any further, Maigret got the photographs out of his pocket and
handed them to the little man.

"What am I to do with these?"

"Just look at them. Then tell me if you recognize . . ."

"What's he done? You're from the police, aren't you?"

He was visibly on the defensive.

"I'm Chief Superintendent Maigret of Criminal Police."

Monsieur Joseph was not impressed.

"Are you looking for him?"

"No. I'm sorry to say we have already found him. He was
shot three times, right in the chest."

"Where did it happen?"

"At his home . . . if you can call it that. . . . Do you know
where he lived?"

"No."

"He had moved into a house scheduled for demolition.
A small boy poking about in the building found the body
and reported it to the police. Do you recognize him?"

"Yes . . . He was known to us as the Dandy."

"Did he come often?"

"It varied. Sometimes we wouldn't see him for a whole
month, and then for a few weeks he'd be in as often as two
or three times a week."

"Do you know his name?"

"No."

"Not even his first name?"

"No."

"Did he talk a lot?"

"He didn't talk at all. He'd sit down in the first vacant

chair, with his eyes half-closed, and let us do whatever we liked with him. It was at my suggestion that he grew a moustache and a beard. . . . They're coming back into fashion again, and our apprentices need practice in trimming them, which is a trickier job than you might suppose."

"How long ago was this?"

"Three or four months."

"Before that, was he clean-shaven?"

"Yes. He had a magnificent head of hair. There was nothing you couldn't do with it."

"Had he been coming to you long?"

"Three or four years."

"You seem to work mostly with vagrants."

"Almost entirely . . . You see, they can always be sure I'll give them a five-franc piece at the end of the morning or afternoon session."

"Did that apply to him, too?"

"Of course."

"Was he friendly with any of your regulars?"

"I never saw him speak to anyone, and if anyone spoke to him he pretended not to hear."

It was close to noon. The scissors snipped more rapidly. In a few minutes there would be a stampede for the door, as in an ordinary school.

"Do you live in this district?"

"My wife and I live here, in this building, on the first floor, right overhead."

"Did you ever run into him in the street?"

"I don't think so. Or, at any rate, if I did, I don't remember. . . . You must excuse me now, it's time . . ."

He went behind a counter of sorts, in front of which a line had formed, and pressed an electric buzzer.

Maigret went slowly down the steps. After so many years in Criminal Police not to mention those earlier years of pounding the beat and policing the railroad stations, he surely knew all there was to know about the human scum of Paris. And yet he could not remember ever having met anyone remotely resembling the man they called the Dandy.

Slowly he walked to the corner of Rue Rambuteau, where the car was parked. Torrence arrived at almost the same moment, and he, like Maigret, was mopping his face.

"Did you have any luck?"

"Well, first of all, I found the bakery on Rue du Cygne where he bought his bread."

"Did he go there every day?"

"Pretty much. Usually in the morning, late."

"Were they able to tell you anything about him?"

"Nothing. Apart from asking for his bread, he never spoke."

"Did he ever buy anything else?"

"Not there. There's a place on Rue Coquillière, though, where he used to buy cold meat or a hot sausage. There's an open-air stall, too, on the corner, which also sells hot sausages, especially at night. He'd go there occasionally, around three in the morning, for a bag of chips and a sausage.

"I went into two or three bistros with the photographs. He'd been seen in all of them from time to time, but all he ever had was a cup of coffee. He didn't drink wine or liquor."

The picture that was emerging was more and more strange. The Dandy, to use Monsieur Joseph's nickname, seemed to have had no contact whatsoever with any other human being. It looked as if he had worked through the night in Les Halles, whenever there was work to do, unloading fruit and vegetables from a truck.

The Chief Superintendent suddenly remembered that he had to telephone the Forensic Laboratory, which gave him an excellent excuse for ordering his second glass of beer that morning.

"Would you be so good as to connect me with Doctor Lagodinec?"

"One moment, please. He's just on his way out. I'll call him back."

"Hello! Lagodinec? This is Maigret. I suppose you haven't begun the autopsy yet?"

"I'll be doing it straight after lunch."

"Could you leave his face alone, do you think? I'll need some more photographs."

"No problem. When will you be sending the photographer?"

"Tomorrow morning, along with a barber."

"Whatever for?"

"To shave off his moustache and beard."

Torrence drove Maigret home to the Boulevard Richard-Lenoir.

"Do you want me to carry on this afternoon?" he asked.

"Yes."

"The market district again?"

"Yes, and possibly the *quais* as well. I imagine he may have been in the habit of sleeping under the bridges at one time or another."

Madame Maigret could see at once that he was preoccupied, and pretended not to notice.

"Are you hungry?"

"Not really."

It was he, rather than she, who wanted to talk about the events of the morning.

"I've just come across the most extraordinary character you could possibly imagine."

"A criminal?"

"No. A victim. The man is dead. . . . He had dug himself in, in an empty house long scheduled for demolition. He lived in one more-or-less habitable room and crammed it full of the oddest assortment of junk, fished out of trash cans and rubbish dumps."

"In other words, a tramp."

"Except that he has the looks of an Old Testament patriarch."

He told his wife about the School of Hairdressing and showed her the photographs.

"Of course, it's hard to tell much from a dead man's photograph."

"But surely he must have been known in the district?"

"No one knows his name, not even his first name. At the

School of Hairdressing, they called him the Dandy. The
afternoon papers will carry his photograph. I wonder if any
reader will recognize him."

As he had said, he was not hungry, and he picked at his
food. He hated to be mystified, and everything he had discovered that morning had only deepened the mystery.

By two o'clock he was back in his office, and, after filling
his pipe, he went through the rest of his mail. Soon afterward, the newspapers were brought in. Two of them, he
noted, had printed the photograph on the front page. In
one, the caption read DO YOU KNOW THIS MAN?, and in the
other, A CORPSE WITHOUT A NAME.

There were a number of journalists outside in the corridor. Maigret agreed to see them. He had practically nothing
to tell them, apart from assuring them that every effort was
being made to identify the man found dead in Vieux-Four
Passage.

"He didn't commit suicide?"

"There was no weapon in the room or anywhere in the
building."

"Can we take photographs?"

"Well, the body has been moved, of course."

"It's background material we want."

"Very well . . . There's a man posted at the door. You
can tell him you have my permission."

"You seem preoccupied."

"I'm trying to puzzle it out, that's all. Sooner or later, no
doubt, I shall succeed. This time, I can assure you, I've got
nothing up my sleeve. I've told you all I know. The more
publicity the better, as far as I'm concerned."

At about four, the phone calls started coming in. Among
the callers were the usual hoaxers and nut cases. This was
unavoidable.

One caller, a young girl, asked:

"Has he a wart on his cheek?"

"No."

"Then he's not the man I thought he was."

Four or five people actually turned up in person. Patiently

Maigret interviewed them all. He showed them the photographs, taken from various angles.

"Do you recognize him?"

"He reminds me a bit of an uncle of mine who has disappeared a couple of times before. . . . But . . . no . . . it isn't him. . . . This man was tall, wasn't he?"

"About six feet."

"My uncle was short, very small, and very thin. . . ."

For the first time that week, there was no cloudburst, and the air was stifling.

It was nearly five when Torrence got back.

"Any luck?"

"Nothing to speak of. There was an old tramp under the Pont-Marie who thought he vaguely remembered our man, but I'm not sure how far you can trust him. It seems that some years back our friend was in the habit of sleeping under the bridges. . . . He was never very forthcoming. It was generally believed that he spent part of the night working at Les Halles, but that was about all anybody knew."

"First name? Family name? Nickname?"

"He was known by a nickname, yes: the Mute."

"Anything else?"

"Every now and then he would buy a candle."

It was six o'clock before Maigret had anything more definite to go on. He had a call from Dr. Lagodinec, to let him know the result of the autopsy.

"My written report will be ready in the morning, but meanwhile I thought you'd like a rough idea of my findings. It's my belief that the man is a good deal younger than he looks. How old would you say he was, Maigret?"

"Sixty-five? Seventy?"

"Judging from the state of his internal organs and his arteries, I'd say he wasn't a day over fifty-five, if that."

"He'd had a hard life, that's for sure. What about the contents of his stomach?"

"First of all, I can now say for certain that he was killed between two and five in the morning, most likely about three. His last meal, which was only partly digested, consisted of sausages and chips. He must have eaten at about two and gone straight home to bed."

"And, finding him asleep, someone took the opportunity to . . ."

"To do what?" objected the doctor. "Couldn't his visitor have been someone he trusted and would never suspect of . . . ?"

"I can't see him trusting anyone. What was his state of health?"

"Perfect . . . No congenital disabilities, either . . . He was an extremely robust man, and unusually resistant to . . ."

"Thank you, Doctor, I shall look forward to reading your report. If you like, I'll send over for it in the morning."

"Not before nine, please."

"Very well, I'll make it nine o'clock."

The thing that surprised Maigret most was the Dandy's real age. To all appearances, he had been a vagrant for some years, probably for many years, and as a general rule vagrants were on the elderly side. What was more, they were a gregarious lot. From one end of the *quais* of Paris to the other, up and down the river, there was hardly a single vagrant not known to all the others, and all took an immediate and lively interest in any newcomer.

"Have you found out anything more, Torrence?"

"Practically nothing. Except for the old boy at Pont-Marie, no one remembers him. And yet some of them have been roughing it for ten years or more. I went into the tobacconist's nearest to where he lived. He used to go there occasionally for a box of matches."

"What about cigarettes?"

"No. It seems he only smoked butts that he picked up in the streets."

The telephone rang.

"Hello! Monsieur Maigret?"

It was a woman's voice, a young voice.

"Speaking . . . Who is that, please?"

"My name wouldn't mean anything to you. Did the man who was found dead this morning have a scar on his scalp?"

"I must confess I don't know. If he had, no doubt it will appear on the police doctor's report, which I am expecting tomorrow morning."

"Have you any idea who the man is?"

"I don't know yet."

"I'll call again sometime tomorrow."

She hung up without another word. Whereupon it occurred to Maigret that he had no need to wait until next day to get an answer to the young woman's question. He called the School of Hairdressing and asked to speak to Monsieur Joseph.

"This is Chief Superintendent Maigret. There's one thing I forgot to ask you this morning. Did you ever do the Dandy's hair yourself?"

"Yes . . . Occasionally, when I was doing a demonstration for the apprentices."

"Did you notice a scar on his scalp?"

"Yes . . . But I never quite dared to ask him how he got it."

"Was it big?"

"About three inches long. And it hadn't been stitched up, so it was fairly wide."

"Was it visible through his hair?"

"Not when it was properly brushed. As I think I told you, he had a magnificent head of hair."

"Thanks."

So he was on the scent at last, even though he had lost it again after only a few seconds. Somewhere in Paris there was a girl or young woman who must have known the Dandy, since she was aware that he had a scar on his head. She had taken good care to hang up before Maigret could ask any questions. Would she call again next day, as she had said she would?

Maigret was running out of patience. He couldn't wait to put a name to the unknown man and discover why he had chosen to live as he did.

The extraordinary collection of junk assembled in the room in Vieux-Four Passage suggested a madman, or at least someone with an obsession. Why else would anyone hoard a quantity of objects that were not merely unsalable but useless?

But Maigret could not bring himself to believe that the man had been mad.

Once again the telephone rang. This was what Maigret had been expecting and hoping for ever since the photographs appeared in the papers.

"Hello! Is that Chief Superintendent Maigret?"

"Yes. Who is this, please?"

Like the earlier caller, this woman—who, however, sounded a lot older—did not give her name, but, making it sound as casual as possible, she asked the same question.

"Has he a scar on the top of his head?"

"Do you know someone who has, and who looks like him?"

Silence at the other end of the line.

"Why don't you answer me?"

"You haven't answered my question."

"There is, in fact, a scar about three inches long across the top of his head."

"Thank you."

Like the previous caller, she hung up at once. So there were two women who had known the Dandy, although, on the face of it, they were not in communication, or else there would have been no need to make two separate telephone calls.

How was he going to find them among five million people? And why were they both so anxious to remain anonymous?

Maigret was quite put out, and he left Police Headquarters fuming. Still, he had learned one thing, which was that his mysterious recluse had not always been that much of a recluse.

Two women had known him. Two women remembered him, but did not want to answer questions.

Why not?

Although there had been no storm, it was a little cooler. A light breeze had sprung up, and it was puffing a few small pink clouds across the sky, as on a stage set.

He decided to treat himself to a glass of beer. He had promised Dr. Pardon to moderate his drinking. But surely three glasses of draught beer in a day could not be called immoderate?

He resolved to banish the Dandy from his thoughts. All the same, he would very much like to know who had tracked him down to his extraordinary lair, and why whoever it was had killed him.

He shrugged his shoulders irritably. He knew well enough that he had no right to expect, as he invariably did, to find out everything all at once at the very beginning of a case. Every time, he behaved as if fate had dealt him an unkind blow.

Then, in the days that followed, the truth would gradually come to light. Was that how it would be this time, too?

He whistled defiantly as he went up the stairs to his apartment.

1 2 3 4

BY THE NEXT MORNING MAIGRET HAD SHED HIS
ill-humor, and once again he decided to walk from his home
to the Quai des Orfèvres. The municipal road sweepers were
moving slowly through the empty streets, leaving broad, wet
tracks behind them, and a misty heat haze shimmered over
the Seine.

On his way upstairs at Police Headquarters, he overtook
a photographer, loaded with equipment, who was on the
way to see him. Maigret knew him well. He was always hover-
ing about when a case was in progress. He worked for an
agency and was prepared to wait hours in the hope of getting
a break. He was a red head, with the eagerness of an overgrown schoolboy, and if he was turned away at one door
he would come in by another, or climb through a window.

Among his colleagues he was known as Coco. His real
name was Marcel Caune.

He took a quick shot of Maigret on the stairs. It must
have been at least his two-hundredth picture of the Chief
Superintendent.

"Have you interrogated any witnesses yet?"

"No."

"Isn't there one waiting for you in the hallway?"

"It's the first I've heard of it."

And, indeed, there was a man sitting on a bench. He was
very old, but spry, and he sprang eagerly to his feet.

"Could I have a word with you, Chief Superintendent?"

"Is it about that business in Les Halles?"

"Yes. The murder in Vieux-Four Passage."

"I'll see you in a moment."

First, as was his invariable habit, he looked in on the inspectors. They were all in shirt sleeves, and the window of their room was wide open. Torrence was there, reading a newspaper article under the headline CHIEF SUPERINTENDENT ON THE SCENT.

That was pure fabrication, of course.

"Any news, boys?"

"The usual anonymous letters. And letters from a couple of our regular correspondents—screwballs, of course."

From his office Maigret telephoned the School of Hairdressing.

"Monsieur Joseph? I wonder if I could ask you a favor? Could you spare one of your young men to go to the mortuary and shave off the Dandy's beard and mous-tache. . . ? Needless to say, he'll be paid for his trouble."

"I'd rather go myself. It's a job that requires skill."

Next, he rang Criminal Records and spoke to Moers.

"Is Mestral in?"

"He's just arrived."

"Would you mind sending him over to the mortuary? He'll find a barber there, shaving off our man's moustache and beard. As soon as that's done, I want some good, clear photographs taken from all possible angles. It's urgent."

No sooner had he hung up than the telephone rang.

"Hello! Chief Superintendent Maigret?"

He thought he recognized the voice.

"I'm the person who phoned you yesterday about the murder in Les Halles."

The young voice.

"You want the answer to your question, I presume?"

"Yes."

"You're not the only one."

"Oh?"

"Another woman called, after you did, and asked me the very same thing. . . ."

"What did you say to her?"

"Come and see me here, and I will tell you. As an alternative, you could give me your name and address. . . ."

"I'd rather not."

"As you wish."

And this time is was Maigret who hung up, grumbling: "Little bitch!"

The long and short of it was that there were at least three people who knew the Dandy's identity: the two women who had telephoned about the scar and, needless to say, the murderer.

Maigret crossed the room and opened the door. His visitor, who was small and thin, sprang to his feet and came toward him.

"I was afraid you might not want to see me."

There was something about his walk, his bearing, and his speech that struck a chord in the Chief Superintendent, though he could not have said why.

"My name is Emile Hugon, and I live in the Rue Lepic, in the apartment where I was born. . . . At the time it belonged to my parents. . . ."

"Have a seat."

"I may not look it, but I am eighty-five years old."

He was obviously very proud of having reached his present age in such good condition.

"I walked here from Montmartre. I make a point of walking for at least two hours every day."

There was no point, Maigret realized, in bombarding him with questions.

"I am known in the district as the Colonel. Mind you, I never was a colonel, only a captain. When the 1914 war broke out, I was a cadet at the Military Academy. I was at Verdun and Chemin des Dames. I came through Verdun without a scratch. It was at Chemin des Dames that I got a shrapnel wound in the leg, which has left me to this day with a limp. By the time the second war broke out I was overage, and they had no further use for me."

He radiated self-satisfaction. The Chief Superintendent

could only exercise patience and hope that the Colonel was not going to tell him his entire life story in the minutest detail.

Instead of doing so, however, the old man broke off abruptly to ask:

"Have you identified him?"

"Not yet."

"Unless I'm very much mistaken, which I am pretty sure is not the case, his name is Marcel Vivien."

"Did you know him personally?"

"He rented the workshop overlooking the courtyard just underneath my apartment. Whenever I went out, I always made a point of passing the time of day with him."

"When was this?"

"Soon after the end of the Second World War, in 1945."

"How old was he then?"

"About thirty-five. He was a tall athletic young man, with an intelligent, open face."

"What did he do for a living?"

"He was a cabinetmaker. What's more, he had had a course at a School of Arts and Crafts. His specialty was the restoration of antique furniture. I saw some marvelous stuff there, the finest marquetry. . . ."

"Did he live in the same building?"

"No, he just rented the studio workshop. He came in the morning and left at night."

"Is there really a very close resemblance between him and the man in the photograph?"

"I could swear it was the same man, except that he was clean-shaven."

"Do you know if he was married?"

"Certainly . . . A woman about his own age would come for him occasionally at the end of his working day. And there was a little girl of about seven or eight who often looked in on him on her way home from school."

"When did you lose sight of him?"

"Somewhere around the end of 1945 or the beginning of

1946. He just failed to turn up one morning at his workshop, and he wasn't there the next day or the day after. At first I thought he must be ill. Then a few days later his wife came. She had the key. She went into the workshop and stayed there a long time. I thought she must be making an inventory. . . ."

"Have you seen her since?"

"She still lives in the neighborhood, and she often comes to Rue Lepic to buy vegetables and things off the pushcarts. For years I used to see her daughter around, too. She was growing up. I daresay she's married by now."

"What happened to the furniture that was left in the workshop?"

"It was taken away by a firm of upholsterers. There's a locksmith there now."

Maigret showed him all the photographs he had of the man. The Colonel studied them attentively.

"I'm still of the same opinion. I'm almost sure it's him. I've been retired for many years. In the summer, I spend hours every day sitting on a park bench or a café terrace and watching the people go by. I try to guess at their occupations, their life styles. In other words, I've trained myself to be observant. . . ."

"Do you happen to know if this man ever had an accident?"

"He didn't own a car. . . ."

"There are other sorts of accidents. Do you happen to know if he ever had a scalp wound?"

Suddenly the Colonel slapped himself on the forehead.

"But of course! It was in the middle of the summer. It was very hot, as hot as it is now. He was working out in the courtyard, fitting a new leg to a chair. I was watching him out the window, and I saw a pot of geraniums fall on his head. It was Mademoiselle Blanche, on the third floor. She was watering her plants, and she accidentally knocked the pot over.

"He wouldn't see a doctor or go to the hospital. He just

dabbed some disinfectant on the wound, and the pharmacist opposite bandaged it up for him."

"Was there a visible scar?"

"He had a lot of hair, very thick, and he wore it quite long, so that the scar was hidden."

"Is there anything else you can tell me about him? Have you ever seen him since around the neighborhood?"

"Never."

"And yet his wife and daughter went on living there? So he obviously didn't take them with him."

"That's right."

"Did he drink, do you know?"

"Far from it. Every morning, at about ten, he would shut up shop for a few minutes, and go and have a cup of coffee in the little bistro nearby."

"Is there anyone living in your block, apart from yourself, who was there in 1945?"

"Let me think. . . . The concierge . . . yes, it's still the same one. . . . Her husband is dead—he was a policeman. . . . She's aged a lot. Mademoiselle Blanche—I mentioned her just now—she's still alive, but in a wheelchair and, so they say, not quite in her right mind. The other floors? . . . There are the Trabuchets, on the third. He used to be a book-keeper. . . . He's retired, too. Needless to say, we're none of us getting any younger."

"Do you think any of them would remember Marcel Vivien?"

"It's possible, but the Trabuchets' windows overlook the street. They couldn't see what went on in the courtyard as well as I could."

"Thank you for your visit, Monsieur Hugon. Everything you have told me will be most helpful, I'm sure. Would you please go into one of the rooms at the end of the hallway, with one of my inspectors, and repeat your story to him?"

"Will I be called as a witness at the trial?"

He was highly delighted at the prospect.

"Not so fast! First we must apprehend the murderer, and have the victim formally identified."

Maigret opened the connecting door to the inspectors' office. Loutrie was the fastest typist in the department. Maigret called him over, told him what was required, and put the Colonel into his charge.

It begun to look as if he had a lead at last. Maigret was anxious to be on his way to Rue Lepic, but he had to wait for the new photographs. Mestral was a fast worker, he knew, so he stifled his impatience and filled in the time by opening his mail.

At half past ten the photographer arrived with a whole sheaf of pictures in his hand.

"It makes him look younger, don't you think?"

"Yes . . . And, in fact, it seems he isn't all that old . . . fifty-five at the most, the police doctor says. How many copies have you made?"

"I've brought you five of each pose, if you can call it that in the case of a dead man. Incidentally, that barber of yours was so overcome that I thought he was going to pass out."

"Thanks. I will need some more copies. I'll have to send them out to all the papers."

Maigret stuffed two sets of photographs into his pocket and handed another set to Coco, the most persistent news hound in Paris.

"Here . . . We've done half your work for you. Pictures of the dead man with his moustache and beard shaved off. Your agency can make copies and send them to as many newspapers as you like."

Maigret gave two more sets to Leduc, one of the youngest inspectors in the department.

"Deliver those to the two main evening papers. Come to think of it, you'd better get a move on. The first editions go to press in the early afternoon. See to it that they get to the editor himself, or at least to his chief assistant."

Finally he went to the end of the hallway, where Loutrie was typing the Colonel's statement. The old man sprang to his feet, as he had done before.

"Don't get up. . . . I just wanted to show you these. . . ."

And he held out the new photographs. The retired military man glanced at them and looked up, his face wreathed in smiles.

"That's him. Now I'm quite sure there's no mistake. He's aged, of course, but it's Vivien, all right."

Maigret nodded to Loutrie to carry on and returned to the inspectors' office.

"Get your hat, Torrence."

"Are we going far?"

"To Montmartre. Rue Lepic, to be precise."

He showed the photographs to the inspector.

"You've had him shaved, I see."

"This morning . . . I've just had a visit from a retired army captain of eighty-five, who says he recognizes him, although he hasn't seen him for the best part of twenty years."

"Who is he?"

"A cabinetmaker, apparently. He had a workshop on Rue Lepic until, overnight, he suddenly vanished."

"Twenty years ago?"

"Yes."

"Did he have any family?"

"A wife and daughter, or so it would appear."

"Have they vanished as well?"

"No. They lived on in the neighborhood for some years."

They took one of the small black Headquarters cars and drove to Rue Lepic, which was jammed with pushcarts selling fruit and vegetables. Number 65B was at the bottom of the road, on the left.

"Try to find somewhere to park, and then come and join me. I'll probably be with the concierge."

The concierge was still quite young and attractive. She watched the Chief Superintendent through the glass panels of the lodge door. Maigret knocked. She opened the door.

"What can I do for you?"

"I'm Chief Superintendent Maigret of Criminal Police."

"Is it about one of my tenants?" she exclaimed, startled.

"It's about one of your former tenants."

"Ah! So I wasn't mistaken. . . ."

"What do you mean?"

"Yesterday, as soon as I saw the picture in the paper, it reminded me of Monsieur Vivien. In fact, I said as much to someone in the dairy, but in fairness I had to add:

" 'It can't possibly be him. Such a respectable, hard-working young man . . . I can't believe he'd ever have sunk to being a down-and-out.' "

As Maigret held out the new photographs, Torrence came into the lodge.

"This is one of my inspectors. Have a good look at these pictures."

"Oh! There's no need. I can see at a glance that it's him. What put me off a bit yesterday was the moustache and the beard. You've had him shaved."

Still staring at the photographs, she added:

"It's knocked me for a loop."

"Do you remember the circumstances in which he left? Did he give notice? Did he return the furniture he was working on to its owners?"

"Nothing of that sort at all. He simply stopped coming, and no one around here ever saw him again."

"Didn't anyone report his disappearance to the police?"

"I don't know. . . . His wife may have. She rarely came to see him at the shop. His daughter, now, that was different. She used to come by on her way to and from school, and she'd look in almost every day, to give him a hug. He didn't live far from here, on Rue Caulaincourt. I don't know the number, but it's next door to a cleaner's."

"Have you ever seen his wife since?"

"Quite often . . . She still buys her fruit and vegetables off the pushcarts on Rue Lepic. Her hair has gone gray, and she's gotten very thin. She used to be quite plump in the old days."

"Have you ever spoken to her?"

"I caught her eye two or three time, but she didn't seem to recognize me."

"When did you see her last?"

"Some months ago . . . closer to a year, perhaps . . ."

"And the daughter? She must be twenty-eight now."

"Someone, I can't remember who, told me that she was married, with children of her own."

"Does she live in Montmartre?"

"I think so, but I don't know exactly where."

"Could I have a look at the workshop?"

"The door to the courtyard is at the end of the hallway. You'll find Monsieur Benoît, the locksmith, at work there."

The locksmith was a pleasant-looking man of about thirty.

"What can I do for you?"

Maigret introduced himself.

"I presume you've come about the man who was shot three times in the chest? Everyone was talking about him this morning in the bistro where I regularly go for a drink."

"Did you know him?"

"How could I? I was ten years old when he left here. The tenant after him was an upholsterer. He stayed for about fifteen years. But he was feeling his age and in the end he decided to retire to the country. That's when I took over the lease."

"Has anyone ever come in here making inquiries about Marcel Vivien?"

"Never . . . But now everyone is talking about him. This morning, while I was having my coffee and croissants, I heard some of the older people around here discussing him. Most of them remember him, and they can't understand how a man like him could become a bum. He was a fine-looking man, it seems, very big and strong, skilled at his trade, and making a good living. And yet from one day to the next he disappeared, without a word to anyone."

"Not even his wife?"

"That's what they say. I don't know whether that's true or not. I'm only repeating what I've heard. Several days went by after he disappeared, possibly as much as a week, before she came here making inquiries. . . . That's all I know, but you want to hear more, you have only to go to the bistro nearby."

"Thank you for your help, Monsieur."

He returned to Rue Lepic, accompanied by Torrence. He was beginning to get a clearer picture of the dead man from Les Halles. They both went into the local bar. It was immediately obvious that all the people standing at the old-fashioned counter were regulars.

"What will you have?"

"A beer."

"The same for me," said Torrence.

There was a pleasant smell of fruit and vegetables, wafted in from the pushcarts that lined both sides of the street outside.

The proprietor brought them their drinks.

"Aren't you Chief Superintendent Maigret?"

"Yes."

"I presume you've come about the man whose picture was in the evening papers yesterday?"

Everyone was staring at him now. It was only a question of who would speak first.

The first to speak was a powerfully built man, with huge arms, in a bloodstained butcher's apron.

"How do we know that he didn't beat it with some little piece or other much younger than himself? And no doubt when she ditched him he didn't have the nerve to go back to his old woman. I had an assistant like that once. He worked for me almost ten years. You couldn't wish for a quieter, more reliable fellow. But that didn't stop him from disappearing one day without a word to anyone. He had run off with an eighteen-year-old girl. And he was pushing forty-five. Two years later, he was seen standing in line for relief at the welfare office in Strasbourg."

The others nodded sagely. It was a typical neighborhood bar in a working-class district. Most of those present were blue-collar workers, small tradesmen, or old-age pensioners, who came in regularly for a midmorning drink.

"Did anyone here ever see him again after his disappearance?"

They exchanged glances.

A spindly man in a leather apron expressed the general view.

"He wouldn't have been such a fool as to show his face here."

"Do you know his wife?"

"No. I don't even know where he lived. The only times I ever saw him were when he came in here for his morning coffee. He wasn't very sociable."

"A bit stuck-up, was he?"

"No, not stuck-up. He just liked to keep himself to himself."

Maigret drank his beer. His first that day. He was keeping count. Next time he saw Pardon he would be able to report, not without pride, that he had cut down on his drinking considerably. Admittedly, the same could not be said of his smoking. He was as dependent on his pipe as ever. But surely a man wasn't to be deprived of all his pleasures just because he was getting on to fifty-five?

"I believe I saw him once on Rue de la Cossonnerie, but his hair was quite white, and he was dressed like a beggar. I decided it couldn't be him and went on my way."

The speaker was an old man who was drinking a brand of *apéritif* that had been popular forty years earlier but for which there was now little demand.

"How long ago was this?"

"About three months . . . No, longer than that . . . It's true, spring was late this year, but it was still winter."

"Thank you very much, gentlemen."

"Don't mention it. Anything I can do . . . I hope you get the scoundrel who shot him in the chest. . . ."

He and Torrence set out on foot for Rue Caulaincourt. Was it really going to be necessary to ring every doorbell and question every concierge in order to find Vivien's wife, always assuming that she was still living in the neighborhood?

Because of the heat, Maigret could not face that prospect. Instead, he made his way to the police station on Rue Lambert.

He had known, several years ago, a man who had disappeared in the same manner as the cabinetmaker, though whether for similar reasons it was hard to tell.

The man had been a prosperous industrialist who lived in Paris and didn't seem to have a care in the world. He was a little over fifty, a family man with a wife and two children. The older, a boy of twenty-one, was doing well in college, and as for the daughter, three years younger, there was no reason to suppose that she had ever given her parents a moment's anxiety.

One morning he had left at the usual hour for his factory in Levallois, driving his own car. Several years went by before anything more was heard of him.

His car had been found not far from Rue du Temple. As far as anyone knew, he had never had a mistress. According to his doctor, he had never been seriously ill and had many years of healthy life ahead of him.

The police had searched for him everywhere, except where he was actually to be found.

He had, in fact, decided overnight, as it were, to become a tramp. He had been to a pawnbroker on Rue des Blancs-Manteaux and there had exchanged his clothes for a set of filthy rags. From that moment onward he had stopped shaving.

Three years later, in spite of the disguise of a heavy beard, he had been recognized in Nice by one of his former suppliers. He was selling newspapers on the café terraces. The supplier, with the best of intentions, had informed the police and telephoned the man's wife, but, although a thorough search was made for him, he was never traced. Maigret thought of him often.

"My advice is to give up the search, Madame. You know now that he is alive and in good health. He has chosen to lead his own life in his own way."

"You're not suggesting, surely, that he has become a vagrant from choice?"

She had failed to understand. The man had kept his identity card, however, so that it had been possible to inform his family when he died, fifteen years later, in the old quarter of Marseilles, which at the time had not yet been torn down.

"Good morning, Dubois." Maigret knew the constable on duty at the desk. By some miracle, or perhaps because so many people were on vacation, the entrance hall of the police station was empty.

"The chief has gone out, but he should be back soon."

"It's not him I want to see. I just wanted to ask you if you'd look up your records, and tell me whether a Madame Vivien, Madame Marcel Vivien, is still living in this district."

"Do you happen to know her last address?"

"Rue Caulaincourt. I'm afraid I don't know the number."

"Is that a recent address?"

"No. It goes back twenty years."

The constable leafed through several big black ledgers, pausing here and there to run his forefinger down the page.

It took him a quarter of an hour to find what he was looking for.

"First name Gabrielle?"

"I believe that's right."

"Her address is still registered as sixty-seven, Rue Caulaincourt."

"I'm deeply grateful to you, Dubois. Considering the length of Rue Caulaincourt, you've saved me at least an hour. I'd have had to plod from door to door."

Although it was a matter of only a few hundred yards, the two men got into the car. Number sixty-seven was near the corner of Place Constantin-Pecqueur.

"Do you want me along?"

"I'd better go alone, I think. It might put her off if there were two of us."

"I'll wait for you at Chez Manière."

There are few Frenchmen who have not heard of Chez Manière, which was only a few doors away. Maigret knocked at the door of the lodge, where he could see a young woman arranging fruit in a bowl.

"Come in."

He pushed the door open.

"What can I do for you?"

"Could you tell me whether Madame Vivien still lives here?"

"On the fourth floor."

"Is it the same apartment she lived in with her husband?"

"I was too young to be a concierge in those days. But I think she moved from a larger one on another floor. Her present place has just two rooms and a kitchen, overlooking the courtyard."

"You don't happen to know if she's at home?"

"It's more than likely, I should think. She goes out very early in the morning to do her shopping. And not every morning, at that."

There was a tiny elevator. The Chief Superintendent was about to get into it when the concierge caught up with him and said:

"It's the door on the left."

"Thanks."

Maigret could hardly wait. He had the feeling that he was within touching distance of his goal and that in a few minutes he would know everything there was to know about the man from Vieux-Four Passage.

He pressed the doorbell and heard it ring inside the apartment. Then the door opened, to reveal an elderly, hard-featured woman. Frowning, she stared at him.

"Madame Vivien?"

"What do you want? Are you a reporter?"

"No. I am Chief Superintendent Maigret of Criminal Police. I believe you telephoned me yesterday."

She neither confirmed nor denied this, nor did she invite him in. They looked at each other uncertainly for a moment, and then the Chief Superintendent took the bull by the horns, pushed the door wider, and stepped inside.

"I have nothing to say to you," she declared emphatically, intending him to understand that this was her last word on the subject.

"I only want to ask you a few questions."

An open door led from the foyer into a sort of sitting room, most of which, however, was taken up with the paraphernalia of dressmaking. There was a sewing machine on a small table, and a larger table covered with dresses in various stages of completion.

"You've taken up dressmaking, I see."

"One has to earn a living as best one can."

Dresses also were piled on all the chairs. Maigret remained standing, and so did the woman.

The most striking thing about her was the hardness of her expression, reinforced by the rigidity of her body. It was evident that she had suffered a good deal and in consequence had turned in upon herself and become, as it were, withered.

In the right kind of clothes, she could have been quite attractive, but she had ceased to care about her appearance.

"Two people, both women, telephoned me yesterday, and both asked me the same question. And then they both hung up on me, presumably because they wanted to remain anonymous. I take it that the second caller was your daughter?"

She didn't answer.

"Is she married? Does she have children?"

"What has that got to do with you? Why can't we be left in peace? At this rate, it won't be long before we are besieged by reporters and press photographers."

"They won't get your address from me, I can promise you that."

She shrugged, apparently accepting the inevitable.

"Your husband has been identified by several independent witnesses, so there is no longer any doubt as to who he is. Did you know what had become of him?"

"No."

"What did he say to you, twenty years ago, when he left you?"

"Nothing."

"Did you notice any change in his attitude toward the end?"

She seemed to give a little start, but her self-control was such that it was difficult to be sure.

"He was just the same as usual."

"Were you and he on good terms?"

"I was his wife."

"Some husbands and wives quarrel all the time, and make life hell for each other."

"Not in our marriage."

"Did he ever go out alone at night?"

"No. We always went out together."

"Where did you go mostly?"

"To the movies. Or sometimes just for a walk in the neighborhood."

"Did he seem preoccupied in the last few days before he disappeared?"

"No."

Maigret had the feeling that she was resorting to monosyllables to conceal the fact that she was not telling the truth.

"Did you ever have friends in?"

"No."

"What about relatives?"

"Neither of us had any relatives living in Paris."

"Where did you meet him?"

"In the shop where I used to work."

She had the pale, dull complexion of someone who never goes outside, and all her movements were stiff and awkward.

"Have you finished?"

"Do you have a photograph of him?"

"No."

"That's him, isn't it, on the mantelpiece?"

This was a young Marcel Vivien, cheerful-looking, almost debonaire.

"That stays where it is, in its frame."

"You'll get it back as soon as I've had copies made."

"I said no. . . . You surely don't want to deprive me even of the little I have left."

She took a step toward the door.

"May I have your daughter's address, please?"

"Where did you get mine from?"

"The police station."

She seemed on the point of telling him that he could get her daughter's address from the same source, but then, changing her mind, she said, with another little shrug of her shoulders:

"She was barely eight years old when he left."

"She's married, isn't she?"

Also on the mantelpiece was a photograph of two children, aged about six and four.

"Yes, she is married. Her married name is Odette Delaveau, and she lives at number twelve, Rue Marcadet. Now I'd appreciate it if you left. I have someone coming for a fitting this afternoon, and I still have some work to do on the dress."

"I'm much obliged to you," said Maigret, not without a touch of sarcasm.

"Don't mention it."

He would have liked to ask her a good many more questions, but he could see that they would get him nowhere. It would take time to win her confidence, if it could be done at all.

Torrence was waiting for him on the terrace of Chez Manière.

"Would you like a beer?" suggested the inspector.

Maigret succumbed to the temptation. It was his second that day.

"What's she like?"

"Hard as nails."

Although he was rather annoyed that she complicated the issue by her stubborn reserve, he could still see her point of view.

Would she want her husband's body returned to her, so that he could have a conventional burial? Had she even considered the question before Maigret ran her to earth on Rue Caulaincourt?

Torrence, as if reading his thoughts, murmured:

"Someone will have to bury him, anyway."

"Yes."

"And the reporters and photographers will turn up in force. . . ."

"Drive me to Rue Marcadet, number twelve."

"It's right around the corner."

"I know. Everything is right around the corner in Montmartre."

It was another one of those districts of Paris whose inhabitants rarely moved. Some of the people who lived there hardly ever left the district, even to go to the center of the city.

"Are we going to see the daughter?"

"Yes."

The building was similar to that on Rue Caulaincourt, except that it was slightly newer and the elevator was larger.

"Will you see her alone?"

"Yes . . . If her mother is anything to go by, I don't suppose she'll keep me long."

He inquired at the lodge. The concierge here was an elderly woman.

"Second floor . . . the door on the right. She and the children only came in about a quarter of an hour ago."

"Does her husband come home for lunch?"

"No. He can't spare the time. He has an important job. He is head of one of the departments at the Bon Marché."

Maigret went up to the second floor and rang the bell beside the door on the right. He could hear children's voices inside. The apartment was well lighted and, at this time of day, bathed in sunshine.

The young woman who opened the door looked at him mistrustfully.

"Aren't you Chief Superintendent Maigret?"

"Yes."

"Who gave you my address?"

"Your mother. I've just come from seeing her."

"Was she willing to see you?"

"Yes. Why shouldn't she be? She's done nothing to be ashamed of, has she?"

"She has certainly done nothing to be ashamed of, but she hates being reminded of the past."

"And yet she keeps a photograph of your father on her mantelpiece."

The two children were kneeling on the floor, playing with a small electric train.

"What puzzles me is why you should have hung up on me before I had time to ask you any questions."

"I didn't want the neighbors gossiping about me."

"Why should they?"

"They believe my father died twenty years ago and that my mother is a widow."

"Nevertheless, I presume that she will wish formally to identify the body and to exercise her right to give him a respectable funeral."

"I hadn't thought of that."

"Do you mean to say that you and your mother would have left him to be buried in a pauper's grave?"

"I repeat, I hadn't given any thought to the matter."

"How well do you remember your father?"

"Very well. I was eight years old, don't forget, when he went away."

"What was he like?"

"Handsome, very strong, and nearly always full of fun. Sometimes he would take me out, just the two of us together. He'd buy me ice cream, and he let me do anything I liked."

"What about your mother?"

"She was much stricter. She didn't like me to get myself dirty. . . ."

"How did you hear that your father wasn't coming back? Did he write?"

"If he did, Mother never told me. I don't think he ever did write. We were completely in the dark. My mother spent all her time looking for him, and she used to go to the workshop in the Rue Lepic every day, to see if he was there."

"Did you notice anything unusual toward the end?"

"No. What did my mother tell you?"

"I could hardly get a word out of her. Was there anything for her to tell?"

"I don't know. I've never asked her, but I've always had the feeling that she was hiding something from me."

"Forgive me, but you are no longer a child. Was there ever any talk of your father's having a mistress?"

She flushed.

"It's odd that you should ask that. The thought had crossed my mind. . . . But, really, in view of the life he led, it doesn't seem possible. He wouldn't have left us for another woman, or, if he had, he would have made no secret of it."

"Did he have many friends?"

"I didn't know of any. No one ever came to the house. He wasn't the sort of man who spends his evenings playing cards in a café."

"Did he and your mother ever quarrel?"

"Not in my presence."

"Have you any idea why he should have become a vagrant?"

"None. Indeed, until yesterday I wouldn't have thought it possible."

"Was he a Catholic?"

"No. He had no religion, and he brought me up to have none. It wasn't that he had anything against religion. It just didn't mean anything to him, that's all."

"Is that how you feel, too?"

"Yes."

"And your mother?"

"As a girl she was quite serious about her religion, but

she'd grown out of it by the time she was married. All the same, they were married in church, purely as a matter of form, I should imagine."

"Do you often go to see your mother?"

"No. She comes to us almost every Sunday, to see the children."

"Does she bring them sweets?"

"That's not her way."

"Does she play with them?"

"No. She just sits very upright on a hard chair—she wouldn't dream of lounging in an easy chair—and watches them play. Sometimes my husband and I take advantage of her being here to go to the movies."

"Thank you, Madame Delaveau. Is there anything else you can tell me?"

"No. I do hope I won't be badgered by a lot of reporters and photographers."

"I'll do what I can, but once your mother has been in to identify the body it will be difficult to keep the newsmen out of it."

"Please do the best you can, anyway."

Just as he was about to open the front door, she added: "Would I be allowed to see him?"

"Yes."

"I'd like to, very much."

Unlike her mother, the daughter had unbent considerably. Obviously she had been one of those little girls who worship their fathers.

1 2 3 4

AT HALF PAST TWO, MAIGRET KNOCKED AT THE DOOR
of the Examining Magistrate's chambers. All the benches in
the long corridor were crowded, mostly with prisoners, some
handcuffed and with guards on either side. It was as silent as
a cloister.

"Come in."

Judge Cassure's chambers were in a part of the Palais
de Justice that had not yet been modernized. It was like
stepping into a scene from a Balzac novel. As in an old-
fashioned school, the desk, painted black, was scarred and
scratched; in one corner of the room there were stacks of
files on the floor. The clerk, though not actually wearing
protective cuffs over his sleeves, still looked like something
left over from the nineteenth century.

"Take a seat, Maigret."

Cassure was barely thirty. In the old days it would have
been inconceivable for a man of his age to have attained
the eminence of a magistracy in the capital city.

As a rule, Maigret mistrusted the younger magistrates,
who were usually full of theories gleaned from recently
published books that they could not wait to put into practice. In appearance, Cassure was typical of the breed. He
was a tall, lithe young man, exquisitely dressed, with a
whiff of the lecture room about him.

"I take it, since you asked to see me, that you have
fresh news."

"I did want to bring you up to date on how things are going, yes. . . ."

"As a rule, that's the very last thing the police want to do, unless they are ready to make an arrest and need me to sign the warrant."

He smiled a little sadly.

"You have a reputation, Maigret, for getting out and around, talking to concierges in their lodges, calling on craftsmen in their workshops and housewives in their kitchens and dining rooms. . . ."

"That's right, I do."

"That's something we are not permitted to do. The etiquette of our profession demands that we confine ourselves to our chambers, except on those occasions when we have to appear publicly, as experts among experts, hemmed in by formalities.

"I gather from the newspaper reports that the name of our vagrant was Vivien and that he had been, at one time, a cabinetmaker."

"That is correct."

"Have you any idea what made him desert his work and his family to become a tramp?"

"I've spoken to his wife and daughter. Neither was able to answer that question. I came across a similar case years ago, a well-known industrialist who did precisely the same thing."

"When exactly did Vivien disappear?"

"In 1945."

"Do you think he was keeping a mistress, running a second home?"

"So far, it's impossible to tell. My men are going through the neighborhood with a fine-tooth comb. What makes things more difficult is that the only people who can help us are the elderly. This morning I spoke to a number of shopkeepers, workmen, and residents, but I got nowhere. This was in the bistro where Vivien went every day for his midmorning coffee. They remembered him well, but knew

almost nothing about him. He kept very much to himself. . . ."

"It does seem odd that after twenty years someone
should suddenly decide to kill him."

"That's why I'm digging as hard as I can into his past
life. The only alternative is to believe that some crank or
lunatic just happened to stumble on him and shot him on
the spur of the moment, which doesn't seem very likely."

"What sort of a woman is his wife?"

"Disagreeable. Of course, it can't have been easy for her
to wake up one morning and find herself destitute, with
a little girl of eight to bring up. Fortunately for her, she
was handy with the needle. She began by making dresses
for the neighbors and then gradually built it up into a
modest little business."

"Did she leave the district?"

"No. She still lives on Rue Caulaincourt, in the same
building where she lived with her husband. Only she's
moved into a smaller and less expensive apartment on another floor. Like other women who have lost their main
interest in life, she seems ageless. Her eyes have that slightly
glazed, blank look that is so often a mark of great un-
happiness. . . ."

"Has she no idea why her husband left her?"

"I could hardly get a word out of her. If she knows
anything, she isn't telling, and I doubt if she will ever
be persuaded to change her mind."

"What about the daughter?"

"She is now twenty-eight. She's married to the head of
one of the departments in the Bon Marché. I haven't met
him yet. She was a little more communicative than her
mother, but she, too, was on the defensive. She has two
children, a girl and a boy, aged six and four."

"Is she on good terms with her mother?"

"More or less. They see each other almost every Sunday, mostly on account of the children. I imagine there isn't
much love lost between them. Odette—that's the daughter

—hero-worshiped her father, and she still reveres his memory. They'll probably be visiting the mortuary this afternoon or tomorrow, to identify the body."

"Together?"

"I very much doubt it. If I know anything, they will go separately. I gave them both the go-ahead to make arrangements for the funeral. They are terrified of reporters and photographers. . . . If you agree, I'll arrange to keep that side of things private. . . ."

"Of course. I can understand how those two women feel. You still have no idea who committed the murder?"

"So far, there's nothing to go on. I don't think, in the whole of my career, I've ever come across a man so completely cut off from the rest of the world. It's not just that he lived alone, in a condemned house, without even the amenities of light and water. It's virtually impossible to imagine how he could have filled his days."

"What does the police doctor say? Was Vivien in good health?"

"His physical condition was excellent. In appearance, he could have been sixty-five, but it seems that he was in fact only fifty-five, and all his internal organs were perfectly sound."

"Thank you for giving me the picture. Am I right in thinking that your inquiries are likely to take some considerable time?"

"Unless something wholly unexpected turns up . . . If, for instance, Madame Vivien should suddenly take it into her head to talk, I think she could tell us a good deal."

Maigret returned to his office and telephoned the Forensic Laboratory.

"Hello! Could you tell me whether a Madame Vivien has come in to identify her husband's body?"

"She left half an hour ago."

"Is there any doubt that it is her husband?"

"No. She recognized him at once."

"Did she cry?"

"No. She stood there quite still for a while, holding herself very stiffly, just looking at him. She asked me when she could start making arrangements for the funeral, and I referred her to you. Doctor Lagodinec has finished with the body. There's nothing more he can learn from it."

"Thanks. I expect you'll be visited by a young woman in the course of the day. She's his daughter."

"I'll take care of her."

Maigret went over to the door leading to the inspectors' office and summoned Torrence.

"Any news?"

"As you suggested, I have arranged for six men to cover the area around Rue Lepic and Rue Caulaincourt, and I have instructed them to question everyone—the store owners, the customers in the bars and cafés, even the passers-by in the streets—in fact, anyone who looks old enough to have known Vivien before his disappearance."

There was no evidence that after abandoning his business and his family and vanishing without trace Vivien had turned vagrant overnight. He might simply have moved to another part of town, or he could have gone to live in the provinces for a time.

It was impossible to search the whole of France. Maigret was pinning his hopes on Montmartre, though he would have found it hard to explain why.

A little later he telephoned Madame Vivien, having looked up her number in the phone book. She had returned home from the mortuary. Answering the telephone, she sounded resentful, as though she had given up all hope of ever hearing anything but bad news.

"Hello! Who is it?"

"Maigret. I understand that you have been in to identify the body. Is it, in fact, your husband?"

"Yes," she said drily.

"Did you find him much changed after twenty years?"

"No more than anyone else."

"I've just come from the Examining Magistrate. I spoke

to him about the funeral arrangements. He says you may remove the body and arrange for burial whenever it suits you. Furthermore, he shares my view that the press should be kept in the dark, as far as is possible."

"Thank you."

"I take it you won't be wanting the body laid out in your apartment."

"Of course not!"

"When will the funeral be, do you think?"

"The day after tomorrow. I was only waiting to hear from you before getting in touch with the undertaker."

"Do you own a plot in one of the Paris cemeteries?"

"No. My parents didn't have that kind of money."

"In that case, I suppose it will have to be the cemetery at Ivry."

"That's where my mother is buried."

"Have you spoken to your daughter?"

"Not yet."

"I'd appreciate it if you'd let me know the time of the funeral."

"Do you intend to be there?" She sounded far from friendly.

"Don't worry. You won't even see me."

"What if the newsmen latch onto it and follow you?"

"I'll make it my business to see that they don't."

"Well, I can't stop you from coming, can I?"

She was bitter. She had nursed her bitterness for twenty years. Was it perhaps congenital? Had she always been of a sour disposition, even before her husband left her?

Maigret felt it his duty to consider every possibility, however remote or even absurd. He was striving, vainly so far, to form a picture in his mind of the character of Marcel Vivien, that loneliest of lonely men.

Most people, no matter how self-reliant, needed some contact with others. But he had not. He had installed himself in a big, empty house that was due to be pulled down at any moment, and he had filled his room with an incredible jumble of utterly useless junk.

He was known only by sight to his fellow vagrants. Some of them had attempted to strike up a conversation with him, but he had gone his way without so much as a word. Two or three times a week he had visited Monsieur Joseph's establishment to earn a five-franc piece, but here, too, he had kept silent, gazing fixedly at his reflection in the mirror opposite.

"The funeral is to be the day after tomorrow," Maigret told Torrence. "I promised we'd do everything in our power to keep it from the press."

"Some of those reporter fellows phone two or three times a day."

"You'll just have to tell them that there have been no developments."

"That's what I have been telling them, and that's what the other inspectors tell them when I'm not here. But they're getting restlesss. They're convinced we're keeping something from them. . . ."

And so they were, needless to say. What was there to prevent any reporter from finding out all that Maigret had discovered?

The following day, the six detectives continued showing the photographs of Marcel Vivien to all and sundry, and asking questions, with precious little result.

Maigret had telephoned Odette Delaveau. She, too, had recognized her father.

"Do you know when the funeral is to be?"

"Hasn't my mother told you?"

"Last time I spoke to her, on the telephone, she hadn't yet got in touch with the undertaker."

"The funeral is to be at nine o'clock tomorrow morning."

"Will there be a religious service?"

"No. We'll be going straight to the graveside. There will be no one there except my mother, my husband, and myself. We'll be following the hearse by car to the cemetery."

Maigret regretted his promise to keep the newspapers in the dark. The murderer, as had often happened in the past, might otherwise have been found lurking near the Forensic

Laboratory or even at the cemetery itself.

Had he or had he not known Vivien twenty years ago? There was no evidence one way or the other. The dead man might well have made an enemy of someone later on, after he became a tramp.

On the other hand, another vagrant might have got it into his head that Vivien had saved some money and kept it hidden away in his room.

This, however, was unlikely. Vagrants seldom, if ever owned firearms, much less a pistol.

In the course of twenty years any number of things might have happened. And yet Maigret kept returning to that day, twenty years ago, when Vivien had left home as usual in the morning but had never got as far as his workshop on Rue Lepic.

Had there been a woman in the case? But, if so, why had he left her later to become a vagrant? Among the letters received at Police Headquarters after the publication of the photographs and the reports in the press, not one had even hinted that there had been an unknown woman in Vivien's life.

That evening, to stop himself from endlessly chewing over the problem, which by now was beginning to sicken him, Maigret watched a Western on television. When Madame Maigret had finished the dishes she came and sat beside him, careful to avoid disturbing him with questions.

"Will you please wake me half an hour earlier tomorrow morning?"

Although she had not asked him why, he volunteered: "I'm going to a funeral."

She did not need to be told whose funeral, and she brought him his first cup of coffee at seven.

He had instructed Torrence to pick him up at half past eight in one of the little Headquarters cars. Torrence arrived punctually.

"I take it we'll be going first to the mortuary?"

"Yes."

The hearse was already waiting outside the house along with a car provided by the undertaker. The two women and Odette's husband were in the car, and Torrence stopped a short way off, to avoid attracting attention. There were no reporters or photographers in sight. The coffin, which seemed unusually heavy, was carried out by four men, and a few minutes later the short procession set off for Ivry.

The sky had clouded over since yesterday, and the heat was less intense. The weather forecast was for rain in the west, reaching Paris by evening.

Torrence kept a long way behind the car occupied by the dead man's family. Maigret smoked his pipe, not saying a word, staring straight ahead. It was impossible to guess what he was thinking.

Torrence did not attempt to break the silence, though it was a struggle, for he was well known as the most garrulous inspector in the department.

The hearse traveled almost half the length of the cemetery before it stopped beside an open grave in a new section, where there were a number of vacant plots. Maigret and his colleague stationed themselves more than a hundred yards away. Madame Vivien and her daughter and son-in-law stood motionless at the edge of the grave while the coffin was lowered into it. Both women were carrying bunches of flowers.

One of the undertaker's men held out a spade to the dressmaker, to throw the first spadeful of earth into the grave, but to Maigret's surprise she shook her head and simply dropped her flowers onto the coffin. Odette did the same, and in the end it was Delaveau who reached for the spade.

He had never known Marcel Vivien. He was not old enough. Maigret put his age at about thirty. He was dressed in black, in what was no doubt the suit he wore at work at the Bon Marché. He was a good-looking man, with a moustache that, like his hair, was dark brown, almost black.

It was all over. The ceremony, if one could call it that,

had lasted only a few minutes. The hired car reserved for the family drove off. Maigret had kept his eyes peeled throughout, but had seen no suspicious characters lurking in the vicinity. It seemed to him, now that the vagrant was buried, that he was further from the truth than ever.

He was in a foul mood. He continued to preserve a gloomy silence, endlessly mulling over the unresolved problem.

Why had the killer of Marcel Vivien not even bothered to slit open the mattress? After all, that was where people of small means usually hid their money.

In spite of himself, Maigret could not get away from the time of the man's disappearance, twenty years back, and that was why he had detailed six inspectors to comb Montmartre.

A pleasant surprise awaited him on his return to Police Headquarters. He found one of the six inspectors in his office in a state of great excitement.

"What have you got to tell me?"

"What was the exact date on which Vivien disappeared?"

"December twenty-third."

"And he was never seen again?"

"That's right."

"Had he already bought his daughter's Christmas present?"

"I should have asked his wife, but it never occurred to me."

"Do you know the Brasserie Cyrano on Place Blanche?"

"Yes."

"One of the waiters there, a man of about sixty, recognized Vivien from the photographs I showed him."

"When did he first get to know him?"

"Later than December twenty-third, at any rate. It was at the end of January of the following year."

"How can he be sure, after all this time?"

"Because he didn't start work at the Cyrano until that January."

"Did he see Vivien more than once?"

"At least ten times, during January and February of 1946. He was never alone. There was always a very young woman with him, a dark-haired girl, and they were forever holding hands."

"Did they always turn up at the Cyrano at the same time of day?"

"Usually between eleven and eleven thirty at night, after the movie theaters had closed."

"Was this waiter fellow sure he recognized Vivien?"

"He claims he remembers him especially, because he never drank anything but mineral water, whereas his companion always ordered a Cointreau.

"It was his first job as a café waiter. Before that, he had been employed as a floor waiter in one of the smart hotels on the Boulevards."

"Did he ever see Vivien anywhere besides the brasserie?"

"No. Julien—that's the waiter's name—lived some distance away, on Boulevard de la Chapelle."

"When did the pair of them stop coming in?"

"About two months later."

"And he's never seen Vivien since?"

"No."

"Nor the young woman, either?"

"No."

"Did he ever hear the man call her by her surname?"

"No. It seems he knows nothing more than I've already told you."

Assuming that Julien had got his dates right, the one fact to emerge from all this was that, whatever Vivien's reason for deserting his family and his workshop, it was not in order to become a vagrant.

He had left on account of a woman. No doubt he had wanted to start a new life.

One would have expected him to keep well away from his old haunts, and yet the Cyrano was barely two hundred yards from his workshop and less than a mile from the apartment where his wife and daughter were still living.

Had he had no fear of being recognized? Or was it simply that he didn't care? Had he told his wife that he was leaving her for another woman? Was that the explanation for Madame Vivien's grim manner?

"I want you to go back there after lunch. And keep at it. There may be more than one elderly waiter working at the Cyrano. The proprietor himself . . ."

"The proprietor is under thirty. He has recently taken over from his father, who has retired to the country."

"Find out where he's gone to."

"Okay, Chief."

"There are hundreds of small hotels around there. I want you to inquire at all of them. In those days, even worse than at any other time, it was practically impossible to find an apartment."

Maigret knew perfectly well that in the end he would not be able to resist going to the Cyrano himself, and roaming around the Rochechouart neighborhood.

He went home for lunch in a taxi, but first he treated himself to an *apéritif* in the Brasserie Dauphine.

At about half past two Maigret stood facing the terrace of the Cyrano, as he had known he would. There was considerable activity on Place Blanche, filled with the busloads of tourists who were bunched in clusters like grapes, with cameras slung around their necks. All of them, or nearly all, were taking photographs of the Moulin Rouge, next door to the brasserie.

The terrace was crowded, and there was not a seat to be had. The waiters—there were three of them—weaving in and out among the tables were all youngish, but in the dim interior Maigret could see one who could not have been much under sixty.

He went inside and sat down.

"A beer."

He had not brought Torrence with him, because he felt somewhat embarrassed by his increasing preoccupation with the mystery of Marcel Vivien.

When the waiter brought his drink, he asked:

"Is your name Julien? Was it you one of my men was talking to this morning?"

"Are you Chief Superintendent Maigret?"

"Yes."

"It's an honor to meet you. I believe I told the inspector everything I know."

"You are sure that what you remember took place in 1945?"

"Yes. The reason being, as I explained this morning, that it was my first experience of the bar trade."

"Was it the end of December or the beginning of January?"

"I can't be absolutely positive about exact dates. Christmas week is such a mad rush, one hardly has time to notice the customers. . . ."

He was summoned away to a table at the back of the café. He took the order and returned to Maigret, carrying two glasses of beer.

"I'm terribly sorry, but I'm alone in here. The other waiters are all out on the terrace. What was I saying? January? Yes, I saw them then, and in February, too, I believe. I'd come to think of them as regulars, and that takes a bit of time. . . ."

"Do you positively identify this man as Vivien?"

"I never knew his name, but there's no doubt that he was the man who used to come in almost every night in company with a very pretty girl."

"And this would nearly always be just after the movie houses had closed?"

"Yes. I remember I was struck by it at the time, though I can't think why."

"Would you recognize the young woman again?"

"Well, you know how it is with women. They're not so easy to recognize after twenty years."

Then a thought struck him.

"But that girl . . . yes, I would recognize her."

"How is that?"

"She had a small strawberry mark on her cheek."

"Which one, right or left?"

"Let me think. . . . They nearly always sat at this table. . . . So, if I saw the mark when I was serving them, it must have been on her left cheek."

He had to break off again, to get a brandy-and-water for a customer who had just come in.

"Did the young woman ever come in with anybody else?"

"No. At least, not as far as I remember. I think I would have noticed, because I had grown accustomed to her face and style of dress."

"How was she dressed?"

"She always wore black. A plain black silk dress, and a black coat with a fur collar."

"Did they have a car?"

"No, they always came on foot. I imagine they lived nearby."

"Did they ever take a taxi?"

There was a taxi stand opposite the brasserie.

"Not to my knowledge."

"When they left here, did you notice if they went toward the Métro?

"No. I had the impression that they were neighborhood people. It's a different thing after midnight, when you get people of all nationalities crowding into the cabarets. But here it's like being in another world. There's a great difference between this side of the boulevard and the other."

Suddenly he struck himself on the forehead.

"What's it I was saying just now? 1945? I'm getting thoroughly muddled by all these questions. . . . What I meant to say, of course, was 1946. In 1945, I was still employed as a floor waiter at the Grand Hotel. . . ."

Once again he was summoned away, by someone calling for his bill.

When he came back, he went on:

"I'm fond of this part of town. It's different from the rest of Paris. There are still a lot of craftsmen with their workshops in some of the courtyards. There are lots of service workers, too, sales people and the like. And then there are the retired people of modest means, who are so attached to Montmartre that they are determined to end their days here, rather than retire to the country.

"Is there anything else I can do for you?"

"I don't think so. . . . If you should happen to remember something more that might be of interest, please phone me at the Quai des Orfèvres."

"Coming! Coming!" he called out to four newly arrived customers, who were showing signs of impatience.

Clouds were starting to gather in the west, leaving the eastern half of the sky more or less clear. From time to time there was a little gust of cool air.

Slowly Maigret sipped his beer, telling himself that it would be his last that day. He was just about to pay for it when the man at the next table leaned across to him.

"Did I hear you say that you were Chief Superintendent Maigret? Please don't think I'm trying to butt in."

He was very fat, very red in the face, with three chins and an enormous stomach.

"I was born in Montmartre, and I've lived here all my life. I'm a picture framer, and I used to have a little shop on Boulevard Rochechouart. I retired three years ago, but old habits die hard. . . ."

Maigret looked at him inquiringly, wondering what exactly he was getting at.

"The fact is, I couldn't help overhearing part of your conversation with the waiter. It was about the tramp who was murdered in a condemned house near Les Halles, wasn't it? I've taken a good long look at the photographs in the papers, and I'm sure I'm not mistaken."

"Did you know him?"

"Yes."

"Have you seen him recently?"

"No. Not for almost twenty years. It was when I saw the pictures without the beard and moustache that I was sure. . . ."

"Did you use to go to his workshop on Rue Lepic?"

"No. If what the papers say is right, he had already left there. Like Julien, I first got to know him in 1946."

"What time of year was this?"

"February, I think. And for about six months after that I used to see him regularly."

"Was he a neighbor of yours?"

"No. I don't know where he and the girl lived, but they always had lunch in the same restaurant as I did, the Bonne Fourchette on Rue Dancourt. It's a small place, patronized only by regulars. There aren't more than half a dozen tables. Naturally, everyone knows everyone else."

"You're sure this went on for as long as six months?"

"I know they were still going there in August, before I went off to the Riviera for three weeks' vacation."

"And when you got back?"

"Naturally, I looked for them, but they were no longer there. I asked Boutant—he's the proprietor—what had become of them, but all he knew was that from one day to the next they had stopped coming."

"Mightn't they, too, have gone away on vacation?"

"No. In that event, they would have come back in the fall. I never once ran into them on the boulevard or in the side streets."

Maigret was somewhat disturbed by what he had just heard. The man was undoubtedly genuine and seemed to have an excellent memory. His story, added to that of the café waiter, pointed plainly to the conclusion that, having abandoned his wife and daughter on Rue Caulaincourt and his workshop on Rue Lepic, Marcel Vivien had, to all intents and purposes, set up house with a very young woman, probably no more than a teen-ager, without even bothering to move to another part of the town.

For two months they had patronized the Cyrano fairly

regularly after having been to the movies. Right up to the middle of August they had lunched regularly at a little restaurant on Rue Dancourt, only a few blocks away.

What had they lived on? Vivien's savings? Was it conceivable that he would have taken all his money with him, leaving nothing for his wife and daughter?

This was something else he would have to ask Madame Vivien herself, since her daughter might well have been kept in the dark about it. Would she be willing to give him a straight answer?

He sighed, paid for his beer, and thanked Julien. Then he turned to his neighbor, the retired picture framer, and thanked him, also.

"I hope that what I've told you will be helpful."

"I'm sure it will."

He filled his pipe and smoked it, walking the whole length of the boulevard. He had no difficulty finding the Bonne Fourchette restaurant on Rue Dancourt. The dining room was small, and the door had been left open to let in some fresh air. Seated at the cash desk, reading a newspaper, was an elderly man wearing a chef's jacket and hat.

It was an old-fashioned restaurant. It even had a wall unit with pigeonholes in which the regular customers' napkins were kept. The dining room and kitchen were separated only by a glass door.

Needless to say, at this hour there were no customers.

"Would you care for a drink?"

Maigret went across to the zinc bar counter.

"I'm not thirsty, thanks, but there are one or two questions I would like to ask you."

"Who are you?"

"Chief Superintendent, of Criminal Police."

"I was sure the police would get around to me sooner or later."

"Why?"

"Because that tramp fellow, Vivien, happens to have been a regular customer of mine for some months."

"When was this?"

"In 1946."

"Did he come in alone?"

"No. He was always with a very attractive girl, and I can tell you, she never missed an opportunity of snuggling up to him."

"How come you remember them so clearly?"

"Because one just couldn't help smiling when they came in. Everyone did, the waiters, the customers. . . . They were obviously so very much in love. Even while they were actually eating, they would stop and kiss each other, right there in front of everyone. . . ."

"Didn't that strike you as odd?"

"Well, you know, in this business you see all kinds of strange birds. Nothing surprises me. He looked about fifteen years older than she was, but there are lots of couples like that."

"Do you happen to know where they lived?"

"No. But I would imagine in the neighborhood, because they always walked along arm in arm as if they had all the time in the world."

"They never took a taxi from here?"

"Not as far as I know."

"Did they ever dine here?"

"No. Not that there was anything unusual in that. Most of our lunchtime customers work in the neighborhood, and go home for dinner. In the evening, we get a different lot altogether."

"When did they stop coming?"

"Around the fifteenth of August. We closed for two weeks, so that my wife and I could get a breath of country air, and I could do some fishing. I never saw them again after I got back. I daresay they decided to go somewhere else."

Maigret thanked him and left. Back on Boulevard Rochechouart, he strolled along at a leisurely pace, as if he were on home ground. He was puzzled. There was something wrong somewhere.

Marcel Vivien had left home two days before Christmas. To all appearances, he had been devoted to his little eight-year-old girl, and yet he had been unwilling to postpone his departure even for three days.

Had he only just met the young woman or teen-age girl he was about to join up with?

There was a telephone booth nearby. Maigret looked up Madame Vivien's number, and dialed it. He recognized her harsh voice as she asked:

"Who is that speaking?"

"It's me again. Chief Superintendent Maigret. This time, I have just one question to ask you, but a great deal may turn on your answer. When your husband disappeared, did he leave any money with you?"

"No!"

"Had he no bank account, no savings account?"

"He did have a bank account, because some of his customers paid by check."

"Did he withdraw his whole balance?"

"Yes."

"Was it a surprise to you when he left?"

"Do you imagine that I was expecting it?"

"Did you know he was having an affair with another woman?"

"No. And I don't want to hear any more about it."

Whereupon she hung up.

In August 1946 Marcel Vivien was still living in Montmartre with his mistress. From then on, all trace of him was lost. Had he moved to the provinces or gone abroad? Or was it at this point that he had decided to live as a tramp?

And what had become of his companion, who had seemed so much in love that they had provoked indulgent smiles from the patrons of the Bonne Fourchette?

Maigret was lucky enough to get on a bus with an open platform. It was one of the last in service. Soon there would be none left.

Contentedly he smoked his pipe while gazing down on the ever-changing panorama of Paris.

What conclusions should he draw from the few facts available? The opening chapter of the story was clear enough: Marcel Vivien, owner of a prosperous little business, with a wife and child, had mysteriously vanished, having made up his mind overnight to abandon everything and throw in his lot with a very young woman.

How long would his savings have lasted? And what would he have done when they were exhausted?

His life had undergone a violent upheaval.

When last seen, in August 1946, in Montmartre, he had been a regular patron of the Cyrano and the Bonne Fourchette.

Thereafter he had vanished again, leaving a great void. Had he grown tired of his mistress or had she, rather, grown tired of him?

He had left no trace behind, but nineteen years later he had been found dead in one of the rooms of a derelict house. He had lived there all alone. He had had no friends. Two or three times a week, he had gone to the School of Hairdressing, to be practiced on by an apprentice.

His murder must have been premeditated, since people do not as a rule go around with .32-caliber firearms in their pockets.

Where was the motive for the murder likely to be found? In those last few months in Montmartre or in Vivien's subsequent life?

There was no way even of knowing how many years ago Vivien had decided to take up residence in the vicinity of Les Halles.

What had happened to his companion? What was her name? Before he was aware of it, Maigret found himself back at the Vieux-Four Passage. There was a constable on guard at the door of the house where Vivien had lived.

He must have lived there for some considerable time, to have amassed the enormous quantity of junk that filled the room. Had he been completely sane or had he, toward the end, gone out of his mind? Monsieur Joseph, the pro-

prietor of the School of Hairdressing, had not noticed anything amiss, but he, admittedly, was more used to seeing
alcoholics and cranks than normal people.

Maigret went upstairs. This was the first time he had been
alone in the dark, dank house, full of weird creaking sounds.
He was not searching for anything in particular. He just
wanted to take another look at the surroundings in which
Vivien had lived.

No fingerprints other than those of the dead man had
been found in his room, which suggested that the murderer
had worn gloves.

Among the junk on the floor was a battered hanging
paraffin lamp. What could he possibly have hoped to do
with it? And there was a pile of odd shoes, all of different
sizes, and a gutted suitcase that had once been handsome
and expensive.

Had he perhaps formerly occupied other rooms in the
house, abandoning them only when they became intolerably
overcrowded? Maigret went farther up the stairs, which were
now very rickety, with many of the treads missing. On the
fourth floor there were no windows or doors left, and the
floors were bare except for a few old packing cases and
cardboard boxes.

He went down again, still ferreting about, and trying to
avoid getting covered with dust. He could picture the old
man coming home at night, striking a match to light himself
up the stairs. The question now was not who he was or
what his life had been in the distant past, but how long he
had lived here, in this way.

He spoke a word in parting to the policeman on guard
and then made his way to the police station on Rue des
Prouvaires. Ascan did not keep him waiting. Maigret went
into his office and sat down.

"I think I'm going to need your help."

"Have you any news, apart from what's in the papers?"

"Yes. But for the time being I don't want it to leak out.
When he vanished from his home, on the twenty-third of

December, Vivien didn't leave the district. I don't know where he went, but he turned up in January, in company with a pretty girl, in a brasserie on Place Blanche, the Cyrano."

"That's no distance from his workshop."

"That's right. He doesn't seem to have made any attempt at concealment. Maybe he was just insensitive. . . . A month later, still in company with the same girl, he began lunching in a restaurant almost entirely patronized by regulars on Rue Dancourt. He didn't leave the district. He withdrew all the money he had in the bank. I may be able to find out how much that was. He left his wife and daughter penniless. He kept on going to the same restaurant until the middle of August.

"From then on all trace of him is lost, until he turns up again, alone and a vagrant, in Les Halles. This is where I need your help. Les Halles is in your jurisdiction. It's teeming with vagrants, not to mention old ex-convicts and elderly prostitutes. Among your men, there must be some who have special knowledge of that class of person. . . ."

"There are four, no more."

"Could you possibly get them to ask some questions for me? My men wouldn't know whom to approach or where to start."

"That's easy. Can you let us have some photographs, especially those taken before you had him shaved?"

"I have a set with me, but I'll call my office and arrange for several more to be sent over to you."

"I can't be sure my men will have any success, but I can promise you they'll do their best. What exactly do you want to know?"

"How long Vivien had been living as a vagrant, which may well turn out to be the better part of twenty years. All these vagrants know each other, by sight at least, and they take an interest in any newcomer, even if they don't go as far as asking personal questions."

"Yes. It may be necessary to go farther afield than Les Halles and question that crew on the *quais*."

"I have that in mind. May I use your telephone?"

When he got through to Police Headquarters he asked to speak to Moers.

"This is Maigret. Is Mestral in? . . . He is? . . . I'd like him to do an urgent job for me. I want five or six more sets of those photographs, especially the ones taken before our man was shaved. They must be delivered today, absolutely, to Superintendent Ascan personally, at the police station on Rue des Prouvaires. Thanks, Moers. . . . Good-by for now."

And to Ascan:

"You'll have them within an hour."

"I'll put my men on it this very night."

It was pouring when Maigret got outside; here and there hailstones bounced on the pavement. The sky was heavily overcast, and the Chief Superintendent was thankful to find a free taxi cruising by.

"Police Headquarters!" he barked.

He was sick and tired of repeating the same questions to himself, over and over again, and getting no satisfactory answers.

He went into the inspectors' office and asked:

"Which of you are free tomorrow morning?"

They looked at each other, and three of them put up their hands.

"You'll have to get some sets of photographs from Criminal Records, and then I want you to go to Montmartre. Concentrate on Boulevard Rochechouart and the surrounding streets, and inquire at all the little hotels with furnished rooms to let. Chances are that Marcel Vivien and his girl friend lived in one of them for about six months. I'm especially interested in the girl. You might also make inquiries in the local shops, the food shops in particular. Good luck!"

He went back into his office, followed by Torrence.

"Any fresh news, Chief?"

Feeling too weary to go over the whole story again, he murmured:

"I'll tell you tomorrow. Tell Janvier he can call off his six men."

He dozed in his armchair for a full half hour, during which time the rain splashed in through the open window and made a puddle on the floor.

1 2 3 4

5 6 7 8

HE WAS IN HIS OFFICE VERY EARLY NEXT MORNING, and by the time the inspector arrived he had already been through his mail. In his opinion, the greater the speed of the inquiry, the better the chances of success.

No doubt the men of the First Arrondissement had been at work on his behalf all through the night, but he was reluctant to telephone Superintendent Ascan, for he did not wish to appear to be putting pressure on him. Janvier was dealing with the various matters at hand, assisted by such other inspectors as were available. Most of the offices in the department were empty.

It had stopped raining. The sky was blue, except for one or two little white clouds edged with pink in the strong sunlight.

"Come along, Torrence, we're going out."

He had no definite plan in mind, preferring, rather, to follow his instinct. Besides, how could one plan in a case like this, with no solid basis to build on and no real clues to follow up?

"The Rue Lepic . . . I seem to remember noticing a branch of the Crédit Lyonnais almost opposite Vivien's workshop."

It did not take them long to get there. Traffic was very light, especially at this time of the morning.

"Try to find somewhere to park, and wait for me."

He went up to the bank counter.

"I would like a word with the manager."

"What is your name, please?"

"Chief Superintendent Maigret."

"You're in luck. He was away on vacation until yesterday."

He was not kept waiting. He was received in the manager's office by a man of about forty, with a pleasant, suntanned face, and invited to take a seat.

"What can I do for you, Chief Superintendent?"

"If you happen to have seen the papers during the last few days, you will have read of the Vivien case. Marcel Vivien was a cabinetmaker with a workshop just across the street from here. This was twenty years ago. I was wondering if you still had copies of his bank statements?"

"Not after twenty years. When an account is closed—that is to say, when a customer withdraws all of his credit balance—we keep his file for a few months and then send it on to the Department of Social Security, on Boulevard des Italiens. . . ."

"And how long do they retain such files?"

"I'm not absolutely sure, but certainly not more than ten years. Otherwise the work of classifying them, and the space required to house them, would be enormous."

"One of your clerks, I noticed as I came in, is an elderly man. . . ."

"Old Frochot . . . He's the oldest member of our staff. He's been with us for forty years, and is due to retire at the end of this month."

"Could I have a word with him?"

The manager pressed an electric buzzer. A young man put his head in the door.

"I want a word with Monsieur Frochot."

Frochot had a humorous face, and his eyes twinkled behind the thick glass of his spectacles.

"Please sit down, Monsieur Frochot. Allow me to introduce you to Chief Superintendent Maigret, who has some questions to ask you."

"I'm honored."

"Do you have a good memory, Monsieur Frochot?"

"I believe I have that reputation. . . ."

"The customer I want to ask you about left this district

twenty years ago, and I have every reason to believe that
before doing so he closed his account."

"Do you mean Marcel Vivien?"

"How do you know that?"

"I read the papers, and since you have taken the trouble
to come yourself . . ."

"You're quite right. Can you tell me approximately how
much money Vivien had in his account?"

"Never any large sum, though of course it fluctuated according to the receipts from his business. . . . On the average,
I'd say his balance was in the area of ten to fifteen thousand
francs. At the end of each month he would withdraw
sufficient funds to meet his current expenses, which usually
amounted to about two thousand francs."

"When did you see him last?"

"It was early one morning, just after we had opened. He
told me that he was moving, and that he wished to withdraw
the whole of his credit balance. I asked him where he was
moving to, and he said to Montparnasse."

"What was the sum involved?"

"Somewhere around twelve thousand, five hundred
francs."

"Did he seem at all nervous?"

"No. He was a man of cheerful disposition, and his business was thriving. Even the very top antique dealers used
to send him their furniture for restoration."

"How long had he had the workshop in the Rue Lepic?"

"Not quite ten years. Eight or nine years, I'd say. He was
a steady kind of fellow. His home address was on Rue
Caulaincourt."

"Thank you, Monsieur Frochot, you have been very helpful. Oh, yes! There's just one other thing. Did you ever, by
any chance, subsequently run into him in the street?"

"Once he'd gone out the door, I never set eyes on him
again. I find it hard to understand how he can have ended
up as a tramp. He always seemed such a well balanced man."

Maigret returned to the Headquarters car, in which Torrence was waiting.

"Did you find what you were looking for, Chief?"

"Yes and no. What I did find out doesn't seem to have got me much further, at any rate."

"Where to now?"

The pushcarts, piled high with fruit and vegetables, were surrounded by a throng of housewives, their voices filling the air with a constant hubbub.

"Back to the Quai."

At this very moment three inspectors were combing the district, going from one hotel to another, in the hope of finding some trace of Vivien. And since this was an area chockful with small hotels and lodginghouses, the search might take days and days, unless one of the men should strike it lucky by accident.

And this was more or less how it turned out. Maigret had hardly had time to sit down at his desk when he received a phone call from Inspector Dupeu, one of the three men on the job.

"Where are you speaking from, Dupeu?"

"From the Hôtel du Morvan, Rue de Clignancourt. Vivien lived here for a time, and the proprietor remembers him very well. I think it would be as well for you to speak to him yourself."

"Come on, Torrence. We're going out again."

There was nothing Torrence liked better than to be out and about, playing chauffeur for the boss. He was delighted.

"The Hôtel du Morvan, Rue de Clignancourt."

They found Dupeu outside on the sidewalk smoking a cigarette. Beside the entrance to the hotel was a fake marble plaque inscribed ROOMS TO LET BY THE DAY, WEEK, OR MONTH.

They all went inside. The proprietor had a bulging stomach and shuffled about on flat feet encased in carpet slippers. He was unshaven. He looked as if he had not even washed, and his shirt was unbuttoned, revealing a hairy chest. His eyes watered, and he seemed to be suffering from chronic fatigue.

"So you are Maigret," he said, holding out a grubby hand.

"I understand that you were here as far back as 1946. . . ."

"I've been here a lot longer than that."

"Have you found the name of Marcel Vivien in one of your old registers?"

"I don't keep my registers for twenty years."

"But you do remember him?"

"I remember him very well. He was a fine-looking man, and pleasant besides."

"How long did he stay?"

"From January to June."

"Are you sure he didn't stay until August?"

"Quite sure, because as soon as he left I let his room to a woman who was such a pest that I had to throw her out."

"Vivien was not alone. Can you tell me the name of his companion? No doubt you also filled in a form for her."

"There was no need for that, since she didn't sleep here."

"Do you mean to say they weren't living together?"

"Yes."

Maigret was staggered. This was the last thing he had expected.

"Did she ever come to the hotel?"

"Occasionally she'd stop by for him sometime about noon. He always got up late, because he seldom got back here before two or three in the morning."

"Are you quite sure he lived alone?"

"If he hadn't, I would have had to fill in a form for his girl friend. The lodginghouse inspectors are very strict on things like that."

"Did she ever go up to his room?"

"Quite often, but only in the daytime, and I have no way of preventing that."

"Do you happen to know her name?"

"I only know that Vivien called her Nina."

"Did she have any distinguishing marks?"

"A strawberry mark on her cheek."

"What sort of clothes did she wear?"

"She was always dressed in black. At least, whenever I saw her she was."

"Did Vivien have much luggage with him?"

"Only one suitcase, a cheap one. It was brand-new. I imagine he'd bought it just before he moved in here."

The three men stood looking at each other. Only one thing was certain: Vivien had left the Hôtel du Morvan in June. It therefore followed that he must have spent July and part of August elsewhere.

As to the young woman, nothing was known about her, not even her surname. Had she lived in another hotel, or with relatives, or had she perhaps had a small apartment of her own?

It was a morning of comings and goings. The previous night's rain had not been succeeded by a cooler day. On the contrary, it was, if anything, hotter than it had been, and a lot of men in the streets were carrying their jackets.

Maigret had not been back in his office a quarter of an hour when the telephone rang. This time it was Loutrie. He, too, was speaking from Montmartre. Two of his men had struck it lucky.

"I'm on Place des Abbesses, Chief. I'm speaking from a bistro opposite the Hôtel Jonard. The proprietor hasn't much to say for himself, but I thought you might like a word with him yourself."

"Here we go again, Torrence."

"Where to this time?"

"Hôtel Jonard, Place des Abbesses."

The front of the hotel was faced with white tiles, and there was a strong smell of garlic-flavored cooking in the lobby.

The proprietor was uncommunicative and somewhat surly.

"Do you remember him well?"

"I wouldn't go as far as that. But I do remember he had a pretty little girl friend."

"Was she registered with you?"

"No. She never spent the night in the hotel, though she sometimes stopped in during the day."

"When did he sign in here?"

"In June, if my memory serves me right."

"And when did he leave?"

"Sometime in August . . . Toward the end of the month . . . He was always very correct, very polite, which is more than you could say of some of the people we get here."

Apart from the fact that she had a strawberry mark on her left cheek, they still knew nothing about the young woman. It was very discouraging.

"You may as well go back to Headquarters," Maigret said to Loutrie.

As for himself, he told Torrence to drive him to the police station of the First Arrondissement. Superintendent Ascan, whose door was open, sprang up to greet him.

"Did you get my telephone message?"

"No. I came straight here from Montmartre."

"I phoned to let you know that we're beginning to get results. Nothing spectacular as yet, but I thought it might be of use to you. Do sit down, won't you?"

Slowly Maigret filled his pipe and, before lighting it, mopped his forehead.

"My men have tracked down the oldest vagrant in Les Halles. He's known to everyone as Toto. Mind you, he's only been around these parts for the last fifteen years. I gave orders that he was to be kept under close guard until you got here. You know what these people are like. Once you lose sight of them, it's no easy job to find them again."

Ascan sent for a constable and instructed him to produce the aforementioned Toto, who turned out to be an elderly man. Though not actually drunk, he smelled strongly of wine.

"How much longer do you intend to keep me locked up here? I'm a free man, am I not? And what's more, I've got a clean record. . . ."

"Chief Superintendent Maigret has a few questions to ask you."

"Where did you live before you came to Les Halles?"

"In Toulouse."

"What did you do for a living?"

"Much the same as I do here. Except that you get badgered a lot more in the provinces."

"Have you never had a regular job?"

He was silent for a moment, apparently deep in thought.

"I've lugged crates and baskets all my life."

"Even as a young man?"

"I ran away from home when I was fourteen. I was caught and brought back three times, and each time I got away again. They'd have had to tie me up. . . ."

"How long have you been in Paris?"

"Fifteen years . . . I've known every tramp there is in my time. . . . I've seen the older ones die, and others come to take their place."

"Did you know Marcel Vivien?"

"I didn't know his name until this gentleman told it to me. He came here before I did. He didn't give much away. He was always by himself, and when spoken to would reply in words of one syllable or not at all."

"Where did he sleep?"

"At that time? I don't know. I saw him occasionally at the Salvation Army shelter. Then I heard that he was living in an old pile that was due to be torn down."

"Did you ever see him in company with a woman?"

At this, he burst out laughing. The question, evidently, struck him as highly comical.

"No, Chief Superintendent. There's not much of that sort of thing here. . . . Especially with a man like him, who —I'd swear to it—was a man of substance. Mind you, we get all sorts. I remember one who had actually been a doctor, but he was a tippler, and he didn't last long."

"Did you ever see Vivien talking to a stranger?"

"No . . . But then, I didn't take any particular interest in him. There was no reason why I should."

"Thank you for your help."

Toto turned to the local Superintendent.

"May I go now?"

"Yes."

Then, addressing the constable, Ascan added:
"Send in the next one!"
"The woman?"
"Yes."
She was a monstrous-looking creature, so bloated that she was hardly able to sit down. Her legs and wrists were grossly swollen. She was more than half drunk, and she looked about her with an air of defiance.
"What have you got against poor old Nana this time?"
"Nothing," replied the Superintendent. "We just have a few questions to ask you."
"What about letting me have the price of a bottle?"
"Very well."
She stood up and held out her hand, preferring to be paid in advance. The Superintendent slipped five francs into the grubby outstretched hand.
"Hurry up, I'm thirsty."
"You told the inspector who questioned you last night that you had seen someone go into the house in Vieux-Four Passage. . . ."
"So help me God, I did."
"When was this?"
"Three or four nights ago . . . I never know what day it is. . . . Every day is the same to me. . . . What I do know is that it was the night they found the body of that tramp. . . ."
"What time was it?"
"Around three in the morning."
"Can you describe the man you saw?"
"He wasn't exactly young, but he wasn't an old man, either. He had a very straight back. You could see that he wasn't a tramp."
"How could you tell?"
"I don't know. It's just something you sense at once."
"Had you ever seen him before?"
"Yes."
"When?"
"That same night, about ten o'clock. He came out of the restaurant Chez Pharamond and stood on the sidewalk

watching the unloading of the vegetables, fruit, and fish. You could tell he was a stranger. He seemed fascinated by it all."

"Was Marcel Vivien there?"

"The one whose picture was in the papers? I believe he was helping with the unloading, yes."

"Did this man, whom you saw again later, at three in the morning, speak to Vivien?"

"No . . . I don't know. You're confusing me with all these questions. . . . And besides, I've got a raging thirst. . . ."

Maigret, with a nod, indicated that he was done with her, and let her go. She would lose no time in buying a liter of cheap red wine, and within an hour she would be found lying paralyzed on the pavement.

Ascan was saying:

"My men will carry on with their inquiries tonight, but I expect those two are the only ones with anything interesting to tell."

"Yes," replied Maigret, as he relighted his pipe, which had gone out.

"We now know, first, that Vivien had been living here for fifteen years and, second, that a man who did not normally visit Les Halles was in the vicinity on the night he was killed. . . . He must have seen him unloading vegetables. . . . Had he come looking for him? Impossible to say . . . Anyway, he was seen again in Vieux-Four Passage at around three in the morning. . . .

"If he was the person who shot him, then presumably, in the interval, he went home to get his gun. He'd hardly be likely to go out to dinner at a place like Chez Pharamond carrying such an unwieldy weapon. . . .

"But, unfortunately, we have no idea who this man is or where he lives. . . . He could just as easily have come into town from the provinces. . . .

"You don't suppose the fat woman could have been making the whole thing up?"

"I doubt it very much. These vagrants are wary of getting

mixed up with the police. They'd only make a lot of trouble for themselves."

"There are five years unaccounted for, between the time when Vivien was living in small hotels in Montmartre and when he was first sighted in Les Halles. I suppose he could have been here all that time?"

"Toto is the oldest of the fraternity. People of his sort don't live to a great age. The School of Hairdressing didn't exist at that time. As for the shopkeepers, their one ambition is to make their little pile as quickly as possible and return home to their villages. I doubt if you'd find a single one who has been here since 1946."

"Thanks," said Maigret, getting up with a sigh. "Your help has been most valuable, which is more than I can say of my investigations in Montmartre."

"Haven't you found any trace of him?"

"Yes. Not only in one hotel, but in two. The trouble is that his girl friend wasn't living with him. She never spent a night in either hotel. So either she was living in another hotel or she had a place of her own. If she had been living with her parents, she would hardly have been able to stay out every night till the small hours. No name. No address. Nothing to go on but a strawberry mark on the left cheek . . ."

"You'll surely end up by finding her."

"That'll be the day! As for the man who dined at Chez Pharamond, he's hardly likely to turn up again in Les Halles. If he's the murderer, he wouldn't want to run the risk of being recognized. . . ."

"All the same, we'll go on looking."

"Thanks again, Ascan."

Maigret went out to the car and was driven back to the Quai des Orfèvres. After all too brief a respite, the stifling heat had returned. Maigret, too, would have liked to carry his jacket over his arm. As soon as he was back in his office he took it off.

"Any news?"

"A woman telephoned. . . . A Madame Delaveau."

Vivien's daughter.

"Did she say what it was about?"

"No. But you can call her back. She said she'd be in for the rest of the morning."

Maigret asked for her number; when she answered, he could hear the racket of children's voices in the background.

"Hello! Chief Superintendent Maigret?"

"Yes, Madame."

The young woman no longer sounded aggressive, as she had at their first meeting.

"I don't know whether the little I can tell you is worth bothering you with, but if you would come and see me soon after lunch, I'll tell you all I know. Don't make it too late, because I have to take the children out for their walk. Somehow I believe that after I've spoken to you I shall feel more at peace with myself."

He went home to lunch. His wife had made him a *coq au vin*, one of his favorite dishes, but he ate without seeming to notice what was on his plate, nor did he say a word about it.

"You're a bit on edge, aren't you?" she ventured. "Ever since the start of this case, you haven't been quite yourself. I get the feeling that there's something nagging at the back of your mind."

"You know how it is. There comes a stage in every inquiry when you seem to lose confidence in yourself. In this particular case, I feel I'm going around in circles. Every time I think I've taken a step forward, I find that all I'm really doing is marking time. And then, don't forget, most of what I want to know about happened twenty years ago. And what's more, there's Marcel Vivien himself, the man who was killed in the Halles neighborhood. I just can't make up my mind whether to like him or loathe him."

"It will all work out, you'll see."

"I will certainly have to bring it to a conclusion, one way or another. Which reminds me that I really ought to look in on the Examining Magistrate."

He returned to Quai des Orfèvres to enlist Torrence's further services as a chauffeur.

"Where to? Les Halles? Montmartre?"

"Montmartre. Odette Delaveau's apartment, Rue Marcadet."

She was looking remarkably cool in a brightly colored, flowered dress.

"Do please sit down."

The children must have been resting, because they were not making a sound and there was no sign of them in the living room. Besides, when Odette Delaveau spoke she was careful to keep her voice down.

"Have you managed to track down the young woman?" she asked.

Now, there had so far been no mention in the newspapers of any young woman. He had considered it advisable to keep that aspect of the inquiry to himself for the time being. All innocence, he asked:

"What young woman?"

She gave him a shrewd look and smiled.

"I see you don't want to commit yourself. I daresay you don't altogether trust me."

"You haven't answered my question."

"The young woman for whom my father left us. I didn't know at the time. My mother never said a word about it. Whatever she may say to the contrary, my mother was very jealous, and several times she followed my father when he left the workshop.

"What I'm saying, actually, is that she knew about my father's connection with the girl before he left us. She never mentioned it to him, but she withdrew into herself more and more. Even much later, when I was old enough to understand, I was not the one she chose to confide in.

"I'm talking now of several years ago, when I was still living with her. I have an uncle, Uncle Charles, who lives in Meaux. He was a big man in the fertilizer business, and he used to come to see my mother every time he was in Paris. When we were left penniless, with nowhere to turn to, it was he, I'm certain, who tided my mother over until she could find some means of earning a living."

Mechanically Maigret filled his pipe, but he did not light it.

"Do smoke if you feel like it. My husband smokes like a chimney in the evening while he's watching television.

"One day I was in my bedroom, and the living-room door had been left ajar. Uncle Charles was there, and I could hear him and my mother talking. I can still hear my mother's voice:

" 'All things considered, I'd say it was good riddance. I couldn't have stood it much longer, living with a man who came home straight from the arms of another woman.'

" 'Are you sure you're not imagining it?'

" 'I followed them several times. By now, I could tell you every detail of their daily routine, and I know where she lives. . . . They haven't even bothered to leave the neighborhood. Marcel is crazy about her. I've never seen a man in such a state. He'd do anything not to lose her. . . .'

"Take note of that. My mother told Uncle Charles:

" 'I know where she lives. . . .'

"It came back to me quite suddenly, and that's why I telephoned you."

"Did she mention the address to your uncle?"

"No. They went on to discuss money matters. My uncle asked if she had any outstanding bills and wanted to know whether there was anything due from my father's customers. I presume you'd be interested in having the young woman's address?"

"Very much so. Several of my men have been searching for her, without results. We don't even know her name."

"I'm sure my mother does. Only, don't tell her that it was I who sent you. . . ."

"Don't worry about that. And I really am most grateful to you. I don't suppose you have any recollection of a very tall, extremely thin man, with a long, narrow face and blue eyes?"

"When might I have seen him?"

"I don't know. Twenty years ago, possibly, or perhaps much more recently."

"I can't think of anyone who answers that description. Is it important to find him?"

"According to one witness, he's the man who murdered your father."

For an instant her eyes clouded over.

"No. I don't know him."

In parting, she shook hands with him.

"I wish you luck with Mother."

He had himself driven to Rue Caulaincourt, where he was kept waiting for some time on the doorstep.

"Oh, it's you again!" sighed Madame Vivien, evidently somewhat vexed. "You'll have to wait in the foyer. I'm in the middle of a fitting."

She pointed to a chair that looked far from comfortable. Obediently he sat down, with his hat on his knees and his pipe, still unlighted, in his right hand. He could hear women's voices in the room beyond, but only as a murmur in which a word could be distinguished here and there.

She kept him waiting about half an hour. The customer was a blonde with an ample bosom and a flashing smile. She looked at him searchingly as she made for the door. Having shut it behind her, Madame Vivien turned on him.

"How long do you intend to go on harassing me like this?"

"You may rest assured that I try to avoid bothering you any more than I have to."

"Very considerate of you, I'm sure. I shudder to think what my life would be otherwise."

"I do feel for you in your bereavement."

In a hard voice, she replied:

"There's no quesion of bereavement. I attended the funeral only because you made such an issue of it. . . . Well, anyway, I did attend the funeral, and now he's well and truly buried. Isn't that enough for you?"

"You sound as if you hated him."

"I did."

They had gone into the room beyond, where a dress bristling with pins was spread out on the table.

"Because he had a mistress?"

She shrugged, as though she considered the question beneath her notice.

"Listen to me, Chief Superintendent. . . . Maybe I'd have done better to speak my mind from the first. For years, Marcel was a man of the highest character, a dedicated craftsman and an excellent husband. He virtually never went out without my daughter or me. Then one day, out of the blue, everything changed. He was out almost every night, and he didn't even go to the trouble of inventing excuses. He went out, and that was that. It was always well after midnight when he got back home."

"So you decided to follow him?"

"It's only what any normal woman would have done, surely?"

Had she ever loved him? Maigret was by no means sure that she had. Yes, he had been her life's companion and the family breadwinner. But had she ever had any real affection for him?

"Yes, I did follow them. I say 'them' because of course he wasn't alone. They were like a couple of kids in love for the first time. They were dazed and dazzled by each other. The girl was barely twenty, and he was thirty-five.

"I guess he didn't realize what a fool he was making of himself. He always had his arm around her waist. Sometimes they would break into a waltz right there on the sidewalk, and then they would kiss and burst out laughing. And do you know why? Because they'd done it again, because without realizing it they had once more kissed right under a street light.

"I followed them into a movie, and their conduct couldn't have been worse. Then they went to a nearby brasserie for a drink."

"The Cyrano."

"So you knew?"

"This must have been in January or February of 1946."

"Yes, January . . . He had only just left me. But I had followed him before, when he was still living here."

"Did you ever speak to him?"

"No . . . What was there to say? I couldn't force him to
come back, could I? Besides, he had become a different man
altogether, one I never knew existed."

"Was he living at the Hôtel du Morvan?"

"You seem to know a great deal. How did you find out?"

"In June he took up resident at the Hôtel Jonard, Place des
Abbesses."

"It was after that that I lost track of him."

"The girl didn't live with him?"

"She had her own apartment on Boulevard Rochechouart.
She inherited it from her mother, who had died the year
before."

"Do you know the name of the girl?"

"Yes. I found out from the concierge. Her name is Nina
Lassave."

"All this was twenty years ago. Have you ever seen her
since?"

"No."

"Didn't you ever think of going to Boulevard Rochechouart to find out what had become of her?"

"It never entered my head. . . . I was too busy with my
work."

Her tone was cold and hard, without the smallest hint
of emotion.

"Do you know the number of the house on Boulevard
Rochechouart?"

"No . . . But it's not very far from Place Pigalle. There's a
pharmacy on one side and a bakery on the other."

"Did it surprise you to learn that your husband had become a vagrant?"

"It proved, at any rate, that they were no longer together.
How long had he lived around Les Halles?"

"At least fifteen years. Probably longer."

"Serves him right!"

He had to repress a smile. She was visibly brimming over with hatred.

"It was very good of you to see me."

"Now that you know how I feel, I hope you will leave me alone."

"I'll do my best to bother you as little as possible. You did say Nina Lassave, didn't you? You don't happen to know whether she had a job, do you?"

"When they first got together, she was still working in a lingerie shop on Rue Lepic. But she soon gave that up. She didn't have to go on being a sales girl. She had an easier way of earning a living. . . ."

"Thank you, Madame."

He parted from her with an almost absurdly formal bow and left her to chew over her bitterness and spite.

Torrence was sitting in the car, reading the early edition of an evening paper.

"Take me to Rue Lepic."

"To his workshop?"

"No. There's a lingerie shop—I think I've seen it—it's quite a long way down."

It was a cramped little place with a narrow window. Inside, behind the counter, a stringy old maid was folding a pile of slips. She was obviously not used to seeing an unaccompanied man come into the shop.

"Can I help you?"

"I am a Criminal Police officer. I'm making inquiries about a woman who used to work here. Were you here in 1945 and 1946?"

"My sister was running the shop then, but she died last year."

"Do you remember a girl called Nina Lassave, who once worked here?"

"That must have been before my time."

Maigret thanked her and returned to the black Headquarters car.

"Since when have you been interested in ladies' underwear?"

"I have at last found out the name of Vivien's mistress. . . . Twenty years ago she worked in that little shop. But the woman who hired her can no longer be questioned. And now we're going to take a look at the house where she used to live. She may still be there, because it was her own apartment, inherited from her mother."

"Where is it?"

"On Boulevard Rochechouart, not far from Pigalle . . . There's a pharmacy on one side and a bakery on the other. . . ."

"I see! You got her address from the woman in the shop?"

"No, she knew nothing about her. I got it from Madame Vivien. She quite literally spat it out. I've never seen such hatred in anyone's eyes as in that woman's when she spoke of her husband and his mistress."

The streets and the boulevards were very quiet. They came first to the pharmacy and then saw the bakery. Between the two was a gateway, painted brown, with a smaller open door set into it.

At the far end of the entrance lobby could be seen a paved courtyard with a magnificent lime tree.

Maigret knocked at the door of the lodge. A trim young woman in a white apron came to open it.

"Who are you looking for?"

"I assume, in view of your age, that you haven't been here very long?"

"All of five years."

"I wonder if by any chance a tenant by the name of Nina Lavasse still lives here?"

"I've never heard that name."

"Does the name Vivien ring a bell?"

"Isn't he the man who was killed somewhere near Les Halles? I've read about him in the papers in the last few days."

"You don't happen to know where your predecessor is now?"

"She retired and went back to her home village, where one of her sons has a vineyard. It's somewhere near Sancerre. . . ."

"Do you know her name?"

"Let me think . . . I only knew her very slightly. Michou, that's it. It's a name one wouldn't easily forget . . . Clémentine Michou."

"Thank you very much, Madame."

And to Torrence:

"We're going back to the Quai."

"What about stopping for a beer first?"

They each had a glass of beer in a bar on Rue Notre-Dame-de-Lorette. Maigret was beginning to see a glimmer of light. Now that he had the name of the young woman, it ought not to take too long to find her.

As soon as he was back in his office Maigret took off his jacket and, standing by the window, filled his pipe. In spite of everything, he was not wholly satisfied, and Madame Maigret would have said he was on edge.

And so he was. He had conducted his inquiries to the best of his ability, concentrating as much on the past as on the present. And with substantial results. And yet he had a nagging feeling that he had missed something. But what? He could not put his finger on it, and it worried him.

"Would you get me the police station at Sancerre, please, Miss. I'd like to speak to the man in charge, if he's there. . . . If not, give me one of his assistants. . . ."

He began pacing the room restlessly. Within the next two weeks, he told himself reassuringly, the case would be solved, and he and his wife would be able to go and relax in their house at Meung-sur-Loire, which, incidentally was not so far from Sancerre.

"Hello! Yes . . . Is that the Chief of Police in Sancerre? Chief Superintendent Maigret of Criminal Police speaking . . . I'm sorry to trouble you personally over what may seem a small matter, but it could turn out to be of great importance. . . . I believe you have a vinegrower by the name of Michou living in your district?"

"There are two Michous here, and the odd thing is that they're not related."

"One of them probably has his mother living with him. She's been there for about the last five years, and before that, she worked for many years as a concierge in Paris."

"That would be Clémentine Michou."

"Does she still live with her son?"

"She died last year."

It was the same old story, one step forward and another step back.

"Would you like to speak to the son?"

"No. She was the only one who could have told me what I want to know. It's about something that happened some twenty years ago."

"In that case, I can guess. . . . It has to do with the Vivien business, doesn't it? How is it going?"

"Badly. . . . Especially after what you've told me . . . I was relying on old Madame Michou, and she had to go and die, a year too soon. Thanks all the same, Chief. . . . What sort of a vintage are you expecting this year?"

"If the weather holds it should be an exceptional year."

"I hope you're right. . . . Thanks."

He had been standing by the window during this conversation, watching fascinated as a string of four black-and-red barges went by in tow. Now he went across to his desk and sat down.

The telephone rang.

"There's someone on the line who won't give his name, Chief Superintendent."

"Never mind. Put him on."

The voice at the other end of the line was muffled. The caller was probably speaking through a handkerchief to disguise his voice.

"What would you say to a really good tip, Monsieur Maigret?"

"What about?"

"About the case you're on at the moment. Take careful note of this: the name is Mahossier. . . . That's all. The rest is up to you. . . ."

And the line went dead.

1 2 3 4

5 6 7 8

"TORRENCE! BRING ME THE PHONE BOOK FROM NEXT door."

Maigret turned to the name Mahossier, little dreaming that he would find eleven subscribers of that name listed in the Paris directory. Which of them was the one referred to by the anonymous caller?

Maigret, having warned the switchboard operator that he would be making a number of calls, began working down the list.

No occupation was given for the first subscriber. He tried the number and got no reply. There was no reply from the second number, either. The third name was that of a florist in Passy.

"May I speak to your husband, please?"

"I have no husband. I divorced him five years ago."

No reply from the next number. In August most of the people living in Paris were on vacation, of course.

His next call was to a secretarial college on Boulevard Voltaire.

No answer. That made four. He got seven no-answers in all, and Torrence, who was standing by the window, marveled at his patience.

He skipped the next number, since the subscriber was a doctor, with an office on Place des Vosges. But he got through to the one after that, a painting and decorating firm on Avenue Trudaine.

"Hello! Whom are you calling?"

"I'd like to speak to Monsieur Mahossier, please."

"Monsieur Mahossier left for La Baule yesterday."

"Will he be away long?"

"At least three weeks. Possibly four. Who is speaking?"

"Is this his home number?"

"No. These are his business premises. Monsieur and Madame Mahossier have an apartment on Rue de Turbigo."

"Do they have a house in La Baule?"

"Yes, It's called the 'Umbrella Pines.' They've had it for about ten years."

Avenue Trudaine was in Montmartre and Rue de Turbigo just a stone's throw from Les Halles.

He began pacing up and down the room. He didn't want to look a fool, especially in front of Torrence, and he certainly would if the anonymous phone caller was leading him up the garden path.

"Put a call through to Domestic Airlines, will you? Find out if there's a flight to La Baule tomorrow morning, and whether it's possible to get back the same day."

Torrence went into the inspectors' room to make the call. Within a few minutes he was back.

"There's a flight to La Baule at ten past ten, returning at half past six. Shall I get a seat for you?"

"Yes, please."

Mahossier . . . Mahossier . . . Maigret murmured the name to himself, with an almost painful effort at recollection. He knew the name. He must have heard it somewhere, or possibly seen it on the front of a building.

He went upstairs to see the Examining Magistrate.

"Any new developments, Monsieur Maigret?" young Judge Cassure asked, in his friendly way.

"Nothing much, except that I now know the name and former address of the young woman on whose account Vivien walked out on his wife and daughter."

"What's become of her?"

"Unfortunately, the concierge of the apartments is fairly new to the place. The old concierge retired to Sancerre, where she died last year. All the present tenants are under forty."

For an instant he hestitated. Then, taking his courage in both hands, he said:

"I've just had an anonymous phone call."

"A crank?"

"I don't know. It's a risk I'll have to take. The name Mahossier was mentioned. There are eleven subscribers of that name in the phone book. Seven are away on vacation. Of the other four, only one is a possible suspect. He owns a firm of decorators."

"Are you going to see him?"

"With your permission. The fact is, he and his wife left for La Baule yesterday. They have a house there. They won't be back for at least three weeks. I have no proof whatever that he is in any way mixed up in this case. But for some reason, I can't think why, I won't be easy in my mind until I've seen and spoken to him."

"You want to go to La Baule?"

"I've made a reservation on a flight leaving Paris in the morning and returning in the late afternoon."

"It's your case, and it's up to you to do what you think best."

"Thank you. I think maybe I ought to have a warrant, in case he turns out to be the kind of person who stands on his rights."

Judge Cassure signed the warrent then and there.

"The best of luck to you, Maigret."

He went home early, had cold meat, salad, and cheese for supper, and spent the rest of the evening watching television.

Every now and then he would murmur, like an incantation:

"Mahossier . . . Mahossier . . ."

But, whatever it was he was trying to remember, it still eluded him.

"By the way," he said to his wife, "I won't be home for lunch tomorrow."

"Too much work at the office?"

"No, not especially, but I have to go to La Baule."

"La Baule?"

"Yes, there's someone I have to see there. I'll be back the same day. I should be home by about half past eight."

He knew from experience that many criminals would have got away with their crimes but for a tip from an informer or an anonymous caller. When he got up next morning the sun was already high in the sky, brilliant as ever, and there was not a breath of air. This was fine, since he did not much care for flying and, indeed, always suffered a mild sense of claustrophobia in a plane.

"See you this evening."

"You might even manage to find time for a dip in the sea," she said, teasingly.

The point was that Maigret could not swim, which was one of the reasons they always went to the country, rather than the beach, for their vacation.

The plane was a small two-engine one, which looked like a toy beside the giant transatlantic airliners. There was room for only eight passengers. Maigret gazed at them absently. Among them were two children, who refused to sit still and talked incessantly.

He shut his eyes, hoping to doze off, but failed to do so. At last, after two hours' flying, they touched down at La Baule. For some time before they came in to land they had had a view of the glittering sea and, in the distance, a single ship sailing on what looked like a course parallel with the horizon.

He hailed a taxi.

"Do you know a villa called the 'Umbrella Pines'?"

"Don't you know the address?"

"No."

"Do you know who owns it?"

"Yes. The name is Mahossier . . . Louis Mahossier. . . ."

"Hang on a minute."

The driver went into a bar to consult the local telephone directory.

"Got it!" he said when he came back.

"Is it far from here?"

"It's behind the Hôtel Hermitage."

He was in a completely different world. Here all the men wore shorts, with their shirts unbuttoned to the waist. Rows of umbrellas were set up all along the several miles of beach, and thousands of tourists could be seen sun-bathing, with as many more splashing about in the sea.

The villa, set well back from the road, a shady avenue, was impressive.

Maigret looked for a bell to ring, but could not see one. The door, which was painted white, was ajar. He could see a terrace furnished with a table and garden chairs. He pushed the door a little wider and called out:

"Anyone at home?"

At first there was no reply. It was only after he had called out for the third time that a very young servant girl in a white apron emerged from the shadows of the entrance hall.

"Who are you?"

"Can I have a word with Monsieur Mahossier?"

"Monsieur and Madame are always down on the beach at this time of day. If you'd like to come back this afternoon . . ."

"I'd rather go down to the beach now and find them."

"Do you know them by sight?"

"No."

"Take the first turn on the left, go to the end of the street, and there you will see some stone steps leading down to the beach. Their tent is the fourth to the left. You'll see the number twenty-four painted on the canvas."

"You wouldn't like to come with me and point them out to me?"

"I can't leave the house unattended."

"How old is Monsieur Mahossier?"

"I don't know exactly. I only work for them in the summer. About fifty, I would think."

"What does he look like?"

"He's still a good-looking man, very tall and slim, with hair graying at the temples."

"And Madame Mahossier?"

"She's much younger. I don't think she's more than forty."

"What number was the tent, did you say?"

"Twenty-four."

Entire families were going down to the beach, already in bathing suits. With some, their skins glowed with health, from exposure to the sun.

He found the way down to the beach and threaded his way through the bodies stretched out on the sand. He had no difficulty finding the orange tent with the number twenty-four.

In front of the tent was a woman. She was stretched out on the sand, lying on her stomach, so he could not see her face. Her back, covered with sun-tan oil, glistened in the sun.

He looked around for a man answering the description of Louis Mahossier. Not far from the edge of the water, where the waves lapped lazily, was a row of some twenty men doing exercises under the guidance of an instructor. One of them stood out, taller and slimmer than the rest. Mahossier?

Maigret did not feel he could interrupt the class, so he stood waiting, not a yard away from the woman outside tent number twenty-four. Wasn't she ever going to notice him? She pulled up the top half of her bathing suit more and turned over on her side.

The sight of a man standing there in a business suit gave her a start. Maigret was the only man fully clothed on the whole beach.

"Are you looking for something?" she said at last.

Her face was smothered in some sort of cream or oil. She was plump, and she appeared to be of a pleasant disposition.

"Madame Mahossier?"

"Yes. How did you know?"

"Your maid gave me the number of your tent. I would very much like to have a word with your husband."

"I'm afraid you'll have to wait. What time is it?"

"Nearly half past twelve."

"He's in the middle of a physical-training class. They should finish in just a few minutes."

"He's the tall one, isn't he?"

"Yes. The third on the right . . . In spite of being so thin—he hasn't an ounce of fat on him—he never misses a day's physical training when we're here in La Baule."

She looked at him inquiringly, but didn't have the courage to ask him outright what his business was.

"Did you just get here?"

"Yes, this morning."

"Driving?"

"By plane."

"We always fly, too, unless we need the car. Are you staying at the Hermitage?"

"I'm not staying anywhere. I'm going back this afternoon."

The physical-training class had ended, and the tall, thin man was coming toward the tent. He frowned when he saw Maigret in conversation with his wife.

"This gentleman has come all the way from Paris to see you. He came by air this morning and is going back this afternoon."

Mahossier was visibly uneasy.

"Monsieur . . . ?"

"Maigret of Criminal Police."

"And you've come to see me?"

"Yes. I have one or two questions to ask you."

He fitted the description given to Maigret of the man who had been seen coming out of Chez Pharamond and who had stood watching Vivien unload crates of vegetables. He had been seen again in Vieux-Four Passage, going into the crumbling ruins of the house in which the vagrant had taken refuge.

"You're in the decorating business, are you not?"

"That's right."

There was something bizarre about this conversation, because of the setting in which it was taking place, the commotion of the beach, the shouts of children, and, not least, the fact that one of the participants was wearing nothing but bathing trunks.

"How long has the firm been in business?"

"I've built it up over the past fifteen years or so."

"And before that?"

"I was an employee in another firm."

"Also in Montmartre?"

"What do you mean by all this, Chief Superintendent? I'm here on vacation. I don't see what right you have to intrude on my privacy like this."

Maigret showed him the warrant, which he studied with close attention.

"What does it all mean?"

"Some days ago you had dinner in the Halles neighborhood, at Chez Pharamond. . . ."

He looked at his wife, as if hoping that she would be able to refresh his memory.

"That was the night my mother came to dinner. Since you can't stand the sight of her, you decided to eat out. . . ."

"What did you do next?"

"I walked around a bit. Then I went home."

Maigret noticed that the woman suddenly seemed a little flushed. She opened her mouth as if to interpose, but she did not speak.

"Yes, you did return home briefly. . . ."

And then, looking his suspect in the eye, Maigret let him have it straight.

"What caliber is your pistol?"

"I haven't got a pistol."

"Take care, Monsieur Mahossier. I warn you that your statement can easily be checked. You had better be frank with me. Otherwise I shall ask the Examining Magistrate to issue a warrant empowering me to search your business premises and your apartment on Rue de Turbigo."

The woman stared at her husband in amazement. As for Mahossier, his expression was stony, almost threatening.

"I do have an old automatic, but it must be covered with rust by now. I don't even know where I've put it."

"Is it a thirty-two?"

"Very likely. I don't know anything about firearms."

"It's too bad you don't know where you've put it. I was hoping you'd authorize one of your staff to hand it over to me."

"What is this all about? Are you going to tell me or aren't you?"

"It's a very serious matter, Monsieur Mahossier. It concerns a murder. When I have found your gun I'll be able to say, within a matter of hours after the ballistics experts have examined it, whether or not you are involved."

"Please yourself. I refuse to answer any more of these idiotic questions."

He turned away to shake hands with a fat man in a bathing suit, who went on to stretch himself out in front of the tent two down from his own.

"Twenty years ago you made the acquaintance of a young woman named Nina Lassave, did you not? And then, through her, you got to know Marcel Vivien. . . ."

"Wasn't that the tramp killed near Les Halles?"

"He wasn't a tramp then. He was a cabinetmaker, with a workshop on Rue Lepic."

"And I'm suppose to have known him?"

"Yes."

"I'm sorry to disappoint you, but I know nothing about these people."

"Does Boulevard Rochechouart mean anything to you?"

Maigret had never before conducted an interrogation on a beach. Mahossier's wife had raised herself up on one elbow and was listening intently.

"Naturally, like any other Parisian, I know Boulevard Rochechouart."

"Where were you living in 1946?"

"It's a long time ago, and in those days I moved around a good deal, staying at various small hotels."

"In Montmartre?"

"As a matter of fact, yes. I worked in that neighborhood."

"Did you ever stay in the Hôtel du Morvan?"

"I can't remember."

"Or the Hôtel Jonard, on Place des Abbesses?"

"I may have."

"Did you, in the course of that summer, take your meals regularly in the Bonne Fourchette restaurant, on Rue Dancourt? Old Boutant, the proprietor, is still alive, and he has an excellent memory, so he may be able to identify you."

"I know nothing about all this."

"You don't know the restaurant?"

"I may have had lunch or dinner there once or twice. Any more questions?"

"Not many. Especially since I'm getting nothing but evasive answers. I suppose you can at least tell me what year you were married?"

"In 1955."

"Did you break off with Nina?"

"You must be out of your mind, Chief Superintendent!"

"Do you still not remember where the pistol is? Can you really not recall where you put it?"

"I'm not even sure I still have it."

"When did you buy it?"

"I didn't buy it. It was given to me by one of my workmen. He had two small children, and he thought it safer not to keep firearms in the house."

"Does this man still work for you?"

"Yes."

"What is his name?"

"Oscar Raison. You'll find him at Avenue Trudaine. He's one of my oldest employees. Now I hope you really have finished."

"I have nothing more to ask you. Thank you for your co-operation. I do apologize, Madame, for having intruded upon you while you were sun-bathing."

She did not reply, but looked up inquiringly at her husband.

In a side street Maigret chanced upon a little Italian restaurant. At the sight of the oven, he was seized with a sudden longing for a pizza. While he was waiting for it, he ordered a plate of seafood and a bottle of Muscadet. They had no half bottles.

He looked grave but calm. He had a feeling that it hadn't been a wasted journey. After he had had his coffee he took a taxi to Saint-Nazaire, where he felt certain of finding a police station. He made inquiries at the town hall and was sent on to Nantes. The police station was rather cramped, and staffed by only three men.

All three recognized him and seemed surprised to see him there.

"Is La Baule in your territory?"

"Yes, but we rarely have occasion to go there. It's just a seaside resort for family vacations. Nothing ever happens there."

"I want a round-the-clock watch kept on a man who is now on vacation there. Is that possible?"

"Of course. Nothing is impossible. But there are only the three of us."

Maigret showed them the warrant.

"We'll do our best to help, Chief."

He described Louis Mahossier and his wife and gave their address.

"If either of them should suddenly leave La Baule, I want you to telephone me immediately, at home if need be."

He gave them his private telephone number.

"Naturally, I would want to know where they were headed for."

"Of course, Chief Superintendent. And now will you join us in a glass of Muscadet?"

"I've just had one. My doctor has prescribed moderation."

He left them and returned by taxi to La Baule. One or two men walking along the promenade were, like himself, dressed in city clothes. They were carrying their jackets folded over their arms. He decided to do likewise.

He took a taxi straight home from Orly. Madame Maigret was waiting for him on the landing. When she saw him she couldn't help laughing.

"What would you look like, I wonder, after a month on the beach?"

"What do you mean?"

"You've been away less than a full day, and you've caught a good dose of the sun. Take a look at yourself in the mirror. . . ."

She was right. Maigret's face was flaming red. And he couldn't wait to take off his sand-filled shoes. He had been unable to resist the childish urge to walk the whole length of the beach, within three feet of the water and its narrow white border of tiny waves. He had walked for nearly two hours, amid a riot of noise and color, with children's balls coming at him from all directions.

"Have you had dinner?"

"I had a snack on the plane. I must phone Headquarters right away."

He was put through to the inspectors' office and, to his amazement, recognized the voice of Janvier.

"What are you doing in the office at this hour?"

"There's been an armed robbery in a post office. It's kept us very much on the run. We've arrested the two culprits and recovered the money. All we need now is to get the third man, the lookout, who managed to escape in the confusion. And what about you, Chief?"

"It will be a couple of days before I can be sure that my journey was really worth while. Meanwhile, can you let me have two inspectors tonight? I want a couple of addresses kept under surveillance."

"We're terribly shorthanded, but we'll manage somehow."

"Write this down: Avenue Trudaine, near the Lycée Rollin. I want the warehouses and workshops of the firm of Louis Mahossier, Painting and Decorating, watched. I haven't the least idea what, if anything, is likely to happen there, but I'd be easier in my mind if I knew that the premises were under surveillance. Next, I want someone posted on Rue de Turbigo to watch the residence of Mahossier. The apartment isn't empty. The old cook is staying there alone for the moment."

"I've got it. What if Mahossier should show up at either place?"

"He's to be followed and I want a report on where he goes and what he does."

Maigret slept badly, because as soon as he began to sweat in bed his face started smarting. He could still hear the murmur of the waves, and the brilliant colors of the beach seemed imprinted on his retina.

Next morning he was again up early and hailed a taxi to take him to Rue de Turbigo. The building was typical of the architecture of the ancient neighborhood. The façade had recently been restored and had regained the appearance of a luxurious private mansion.

"Excuse me, Madame. Can you please direct me to Monsieur Mahossier's apartment?"

"He's not here. He and his wife are on vacation at their villa in La Baule."

"I know. But I understand that their cook, Mademoiselle Berthe, is in residence."

"Oh, very well. It's one floor up, the door on the right—though in fact either door would do, since their place occupies the whole floor."

There was no elevator, but the staircase was wide, with shallow treads. The door was of old wood gleaming with wax polish. He rang, and was kept waiting for some time before anything happened. Eventually he heard light footsteps approaching, and the door was opened.

"Monsieur and Madame Mahossier are . . ."

"They're in La Baule, I know. It's you I've come to see."

"Me?"

"Yes. You are Mademoiselle Berthe, the cook, are you not?"

"Come in. There's no point in hanging around here on the landing."

She led him into the vast drawing room, which was lighted by three tall windows. Most of the furniture was contemporary with the house.

"Please sit down. Are you a vacuum-cleaner salesman?"

"No. I'm from Criminal Police."

She gave him a long bold stare. She was obviously not without courage and surely would not hestitate to speak her mind.

"You're Chief Superintendent Maigret, aren't you?"

"Yes."

"You're in charge of that murder case. . . . The tramp . . . what was his name? I can't remember names as I used to."

"Vivien."

"Yes. What an extraordinary thing to do, to kill a tramp, don't you think? Unless he was one of those who kept a fortune sewed up in his mattress."

"He wasn't. I saw your employer yesterday in La Baule."

"Oh?"

"Did you know him before he was married?"

"Well, I first met him when he became engaged to Mademoiselle Cassegrain. At that time, I was in service with her parents. Monsieur Cassegrain is a notary. He lives on Avenue de Villiers. His wife is in very poor health. She had a personal maid who looked after her and did the cooking.

"It was Monsieur Cassegrain who persuaded me to go with his daughter when she got married."

"How long ago was that?"

"About ten years. The only difference in this place is that Madame has no personal maid, and I have to do everything myself. Well, perhaps that's not quite fair. Madame helps me a lot, and she's as good a cook as I am. . . ."

"Do they go out a lot?"

"Very rarely. Just occasionally to the theater or the movies. They hardly ever entertain, except for one or two close friends."

"Do they get along well together?"

"They don't argue over every little thing, if that's what you mean."

"Do you think they are still fond of each other?"

Her reply to this was an eloquent silence.

"Has Monsieur Mahossier a mistress?"

"I've no idea. He'd hardly be likely to tell me if he did."

"Does he ever go out alone at night and come home very late?"

"Never . . . At least, not until one night last week. . . . It was about eleven o'clock. Madame had had her mother to dinner here and was driving her home. He rushed in like a whirlwind and made straight for his bedroom. And then he went out again, as suddenly as he had come in. When Madame returned, she decided not to wait up for him and went straight to bed. I don't know whether she heard him come in, he crept in so quietly, but I did. . . . And I can tell you that it was past three o'clock in the morning."

"How long have they had separate bedrooms?"

"Almost since they were first married. Monsieur has to be up very early in the morning, to supervise his workmen. Madame, who likes to sleep late, found that it disturbed her."

One only had to hear her allude to Mahossier to realize that she disliked him, whereas she spoke of her mistress with positive adoration.

"How old was she when she married?"

"It was just a month after her twentieth birthday."

"Do you happen to know where they met?"

"No. She went out a lot before she was married. And, as you know, girls nowadays go everywhere unchaperoned."

"Is she happy?"

Another eloquent silence.

"Has her marriage been a disappointment to her?"

"She's not the kind of woman to complain or go into a decline. She takes things as they come."

Maigret noticed that there was a photograph of the Mahossiers on the piano. Louis Mahossier was wearing a moustache, which he had since shaved off, and the young woman had blond curls all over her head.

The cook, following Maigret's glance, abruptly asked:

"What's he done?"

"Why do you ask? He hasn't necessarily done anything."

"In that case you wouldn't be here. When a man like you takes the trouble . . ."

"Would you show me his bedroom?"

"He'd be furious if he knew, but I don't care. I'm not afraid of him."

They went through the dining room and out into a hallway.

"Here," she said, flinging open a door. "This is Madame's bedroom."

It was a cheerful room. The color scheme was pale gray with touches of blue. The floor was covered with a white carpet. Maigret felt his feet sinking into it.

Mahossier's room, adjoining, was more subdued, naturally, but everything was in the best of taste.

"Who chose the color schemes and the furniture?"

"Madame. She took a course in art history at the Louvre, and another at the School of Interior Design."

"Is she the one who plays the piano?"

"Yes, but only when she's home alone."

The room they were in now was done in soft shades of beige and brown.

"Tell me, does Mahossier own a pistol?"

"Yes. I saw it recently, about two weeks ago."

"Is it a revolver?"

"Does that mean it has a kind of cylinder to hold the bullets?"

"Yes."

"No. It's quite flat."

"An automatic."

"You can see for yourself."

She went to the bedside table and opened the top drawer. A look of shocked bewilderment came into her face.

"It's not here."

"Perhaps he took it with him to La Baule?"

"No, he didn't. I packed the suitcases myself."

"Could he have put it somewhere else?"

She opened the two other drawers, which contained keys, a penknife, and a number of club membership cards.

"It's been in this same drawer ever since I came to this house."

"And you say you saw it as recently as two weeks ago? ... Were there any cartridges with it?"

"A whole boxful. They're gone, too."

She looked in all the closets and drawers, and even searched in the bathroom.

When she came face to face with Maigret again she looked grave and a little pale.

"I think I'm beginning to see why you're here."

"Does it surprise you?"

"A little. Not all that much. If I tell you why, I guess you'll laugh at me. He doesn't like animals. He won't have a dog or a cat in the place. Madame used to have a cocker spaniel—it was company for her—but he made her get rid of it."

"I'd be grateful if you would remain in Paris for the next few days. I may be needing you very soon now."

"I'll be here."

And, after a slight pause, as they were on the way back to the drawing room:

"Did you see Madame in La Baule?"

"Yes."

"I bet you she was sun-bathing."

"She was."

"When she's at the beach she spends every minute she can soaking up the sun. She used to go to La Baule with her parents, as a child."

"Don't they want any children?"

"They've never discussed it with me, but I don't think they're all that anxious to."

"Many thanks, Mademoiselle Berthe. You have been most helpful."

"I did my best, I'm sure. . . ."

But she did not add:

"And I also did my best to land my employer in the soup."

He returned by taxi to the Quai des Orfèvres. Torrence announced that there had been a phone call from Nantes reporting there was nothing new at the villa so picturesquely named the "Umbrella Pines." They wanted to know if they were to keep up the watch.

"Call them back and say yes."

He found Janvier in the inspectors' office.

"Have you posted the two men, as I asked?"

Janvier was the only one whom he regularly addressed by the familiar *tu*, though occasionally he did the same speaking to young Lapointe, the most junior of the inspectors. With the others, he normally stuck to the more formal *vous*, except in moments of absent-mindedness or stress.

"Whom have you sent to Rue de Turbigo? Whoever it is is keeping himself well hidden. I've just come from there, and I didn't see anyone. True, there is a bistro just opposite the house."

"Baron is there, and Neveu went to Montmartre."

Maigret went across to the wing that housed the examining magistrates and knocked at Judge Cassure's door.

"Come in," the judge called out.

"Are you making any progress?"

"In a way, yes. As a matter of fact, I would like to ask you to sign a warrant authorizing me to keep my man under surveillance."

"Tell me about it."

Maigret dropped into an uncomfortable chair and began giving the details of his peregrinations in the course of the past two days.

"I can't guarantee that Mahossier is the murderer of Vivien, but I have enough evidence to justify a more searching interrogation than I was able to carry out on the beach. . . ."

"I agree with you. . . . How are you going to set about it? Are you going to send two men down there to arrest him, or will you leave it to the local police?"

"I'll send two of my own men if they can possibly be spared. We're so short-staffed at the moment that if the criminal fraternity got wind of it they would have a field day."

"I'll sign a surveillance warrant right away."

He began filling in one of the forms so familiar to Maigret.

"First name?"

"Louis."

"Is there an *h* in Mahossier? I don't know why, but I seem to have an itch to spell it Marossier."

"Thanks, Judge."

"Have you been to Avenue Trudaine?"

"I intend to go there this morning."

Returning to his own floor, he sought out Janvier.

"Look, I absolutely must have two more men. . . ."

Poor Janvier did not know which way to turn.

"Will you need them for long?"

"Just long enough to bring someone back from La Baule."

He looked searchingly at Maigret and understanding began to dawn.

"I get it! You can have Véran and Loubet. . . ."

Maigret took both the men into his office, gave them instructions, and then handed them the surveillance warrant.

"There's a plane leaving in an hour. You should be able to catch it. But I would prefer you to return by train."

"Is he to be handcuffed?"

"Only if he tries to give you the slip. Otherwise, I don't think it will be necessary."

He called out to Torrence:

"Come on. I'm needing my chauffeur again."

In point of fact, Torrence had been pretty much his full-time chauffeur for the past few days.

"Avenue Trudaine . . . Just opposite the Lycée Rollin . . ."

"Are you having him arrested?"

"I'm bringing him in for questioning. We'll see how things go after I've put him through it a bit more thoroughly than I was able to do on the beach."

He found himself in a large courtyard, with ladders lying all over the place and, at the end, a kind of garage full of huge drums of paint. An enamel plaque inscribed OFFICE, with an arrow, directed Maigret to the place he was seeking.

The office turned out to be a single fairly large room, whose sole occupant was a grumpy-looking little man bent over a stack of invoices.

"I am Chief Superintendent Maigret."

"Are you sure it's me you're looking for?"

"What is your name?"

"Vannier . . . Gérard Vannier. And I can't imagine what the police can . . ."

"It doesn't concern you personally."

"Is it one of our workmen? They're all out on various jobs. And besides, they're all reliable men, who have been with us for years."

"Does that door there on the left lead to the boss's office?"

"Yes, but he's hardly ever in it. He's always at one or another of the jobs."

"Is it a profitable business?"

"We have nothing to complain about."

"Are you a partner?"

"Alas, no. I'm just the bookkeeper."

"How long has the business been going?"

"That I can't tell you. All I know is that the former owner went broke in 1947. It's true, he spent most of his time in one bistro or another, and there was a good deal of waste. Anyway, Monsieur Mahossier took over the business and fired all the old staff."

"What about you?"

"At first a bookkeeper was needed only two days a week. Then, as business started to pick up, he took me on full time. This was toward the end of 1948."

"Is he a hard worker?"

"He keeps an eye on every detail of the business. Some days he barely has time to slip out for a quick lunch."

"How does he get on with his workmen?"

"He's very friendly with all of them, but he knows where to draw the line, and they respect it."

"How many workmen does he employ?"

"At the moment, eight, including one apprentice."

"Do you know if he keeps a pistol in his office?"

"A pistol? No. Why ever should he? Most of his customers pay by check, and those are taken straight to the bank on the corner of the Avenue."

"Do you mind?"

To the man's intense indignation, Maigret went into Mahossier's office and opened all the drawers, one after the other. There was no gun in any of them.

"What, precisely, are you here for?"

"I'm conducting an inquiry."

"When Monsieur Mahossier hears about this . . ."

"I saw him yesterday."

"You mean you went all the way to La Baule?"

"Yes, and by tomorrow morning, at the latest, he will be back in Paris."

"He was planning to be away for three weeks or a month."

"I persuaded him to change his mind."

"Didn't he object?"

The little fellow's hackles were up, and no mistake. He looked like a fighting cock about to strike.

"I'd very much like to know what all this is about."

"You'll find out soon enough."

"Making yourself at home in the boss's office . . . Opening drawers . . . Asking silly questions . . . And now telling me that you have persuaded the boss to return from La Baule . . ."

Maigret, without saying another word, left the little fellow to fulminate in solitude.

1234

NO SOONER WAS MAIGRET BACK AT THE QUAI DES
Orfèvres than he received a telephone call from La Baule. It
was from Véran, one of the two inspectors sent to bring
Mahossier back to Paris.

"How did it go?"

"Not too good, to begin with. At first he got on his high
horse and refused to come with us to Paris. He spoke about
friends in high places and threatened big trouble for the
department."

"How did his wife take it?"

"She just listened. She was obviously surprised. I gave
them a few minutes to talk it over. Then I took the hand-
cuffs out of my pocket and told him that if he didn't come
quietly he'd find himself wearing them all the way to Paris.
He was furious."

"Would you have actually had the nerve to do that?"

"Yes."

"But why, in God's name?"

"I realized that what he dreaded more than anything was
public humiliation. At any rate, he eventually agreed to
come with us to the station and catch the night train. His
wife wanted to come, too, but he wouldn't have it. He told
her he'd be back within forty-eight hours.

" 'I tell you, they've got nothing on me. They're only
storing up trouble for themselves.' "

Next morning, Maigret went straight into the office. He sat down at his desk, chose a pipe, and filled it with great deliberation. Then he summoned Torrence and told him to sit at one end of the desk, ready to take shorthand notes. It was usually Lapointe, the most highly skilled stenographer in the department, who took down statements, but Torrence was competent enough.

Maigret pressed a buzzer, and Véran appeared with Mahossier, who gave him a hard, unwavering stare.

"Sit down, please."

"I protest. I have been wrongfully arrested, and I reserve the right to bring an action against you, even though you are the great Maigret himself."

Maigret was impassive.

"Would you kindly tell me, Monsieur Mahossier, where your pistol is to be found?"

"What pistol?"

"The one that until only a few days ago was kept in the top drawer of your bedside table. A thirty-two, if I'm not mistaken."

"I know nothing about firearms, and I couldn't tell you what caliber this one was. As I said before, it was given to me a long time ago."

"Where is it now?"

"Where it always has been, I would guess."

He spoke snappishly, and looked with eyes full of hatred at the Chief Superintendent. But was there not also a hint of fear in those eyes?

"The pistol is no longer in the drawer. What have you done with it?"

"I'm not the only person with access to the apartment."

"Are you suggesting that Mademoiselle Berthe might have taken it? All I can say to that is that flippancy will get you nowhere."

"I wasn't suggesting that the cook had taken it. . . ."

"Who, then? Your mother-in-law, perhaps? After all, she was in your apartment on the night you dined alone at Chez Pharamond and returned home at three in the morning."

"I have never returned home as late as three in the morning."

"Do you wish me to confront you with the witness who saw you clearly, and who will not hesitate to identify you?"

Torrence, his forehead bathed in sweat, was scribbling away as fast as he could.

"Not only do we have a witness who saw you go down Vieux-Four Passage shortly before three, but there is another witness who heard you coming into your apartment a few minutes after three."

Sardonically he said:

"Are you by any chance referring to my wife?"

"If it were your wife, she could not testify against you."

In contrast to his suspect, Maigret was very composed.

"Then it must have been that old bitch, Berthe. Just because she brought up my wife more or less singlehanded, she's so jealous of anyone else at all close to her that she can't stand the sight of me."

"Where did you first meet Marcel Vivien?"

"I don't know anyone of that name."

"Don't you read the papers?"

"I don't pay much attention to the news items."

"All the same, you do know that he was murdered? He was asleep in his bed when he was shot three times in the chest."

"What does that have to do with me?"

"It may have a great deal to do with you. It would be a great help if you could produce your pistol."

"First, I'd need to know who had moved it or stolen it."

He was the sort of man who would go on protesting his innocence in the teeth of the strongest evidence. He lighted a cigarette with trembling fingers. He might have been trembling with rage.

"Are you saying that you've never been in Vieux-Four Passage?"

"I don't even know where it is."

Abruptly Maigret changed the subject, to the discomfiture of his suspect.

"What happened to Nina Lassave?"

"Am I supposed to know her? The name means absolutely nothing to me."

"In 1945 and '46 you lived in Montmartre, in a private hotel, a mere stone's throw from Boulevard Rochechouart."

"I did live around there at one time, but I can't remember what year it was."

"The girl in question had an apartment on Boulevard Rochechouart."

"Maybe she did. But then, so do thousands of others. Am I supposed to know every one of them?"

"The probability is that you did make her acquaintance, as well as that of Marcel Vivien, who was her lover at the time. Please take time for reflection before you answer my next question. Were you, also, Nina Lassave's lover?"

"I don't need time for reflection. The answer is no. During that period, which was before my marriage, I did have a succession of mistresses, but no one of that name, and I never knew anyone called Marcel Vivien."

"In other words, you have no connection with anyone concerned in this case?"

"None whatsoever."

He was growing bolder, yet at the same time he was noticeably more tense, and he could not prevent his hands from trembling.

"I am sending you back to your cell, to give you time to think things over."

"By what right . . . ?"

"Aren't you forgetting the warrant for your arrest, duly signed by the Examining Magistrate?"

"If you insist on putting me through another interrogation, I demand that my lawyer be present."

"I would be within my rights to refuse at this stage. It is not until the Examining Magistrate takes over that you become entitled to legal representation. But I don't wish to be obstructive. What's your lawyer's name?"

"Maître Loiseau. His address is number thirty-eight, Boulevard Beaumarchais."

"I'll let him know in good time."

Maigret got up, lumbered over to the open window, and gazed out at the glaringly blue sky. Everyone, except for those who were at the seaside, was longing for the rain, which persisted in holding off. The temperature was still rising.

Inspector Véran took Mahossier back to his cell.

"He won't be getting away with this," muttered Mahossier under his breath, no doubt referring to Chief Superintendent Maigret.

Maigret, for his part, was remarking to Torrence:

"He's very stubborn. Get those notes of yours typed up, will you? I'll get him to sign his statement next time."

"Do you really believe he knew Nina Lassave?"

"It's a possibility. It was only a stab in the dark. I thought I detected some reaction. He certainly wasn't expecting me to mention her name. . . ."

He chose a fresh pipe from the rack and put on his hat.

"If I'm wanted for anything urgent, I'll be at the office of the *Parisien Libéré.* . . ."

Torrence looked surprised, but said nothing. First Maigret stopped off at the Brasserie Dauphine for a glass of beer. Then he got into a taxi.

"To the office of the *Parisien Libéré.* . . ."

He recalled that this was one of the first newspapers to appear after the Liberation. He himself had been out of Paris in 1946. Shortly before, he had fallen out with the then Chief Commissioner of Police, who had retired a few months later. He had been posted to Luçon, where there had been practically nothing to do, and to pass the time he had spent most of the day playing billiards. He had had to stay there, bored and frustrated, for the better part of a year. Nor had Madame Maigret taken to life in the Vendée.

Fortunately, the new Commissioner had summoned him back to Paris. At the time Maigret was only an inspector. He had not yet been promoted to Chief Superintendent and head of Criminal Police. Maigret now looked back on his time in Luçon as not merely a gap in his career, but also a blank in his memory.

"I would like to see the editor."

"Your name, please."

"Chief Superintèndent Maigret."

The editor, whom he had never met before, and who turned out to be quite a young man, came out of his office to greet him.

"What an honor to see you here, Monsieur; what's it about?"

"It's about a case I'm working on," Maigret explained.

"What can we do to help you?"

"I presume you have files of all the back numbers of your paper?"

"Of course. They are bound and arranged in chronological order."

"I'd like to look up the years 1945 and '46."

"This way, please."

He followed the editor through a bewildering maze of hallways and came at last to a dark room fitted with bookshelves filled with rows of huge volumes bound in black cloth.

"Do you need any help? I could let you have someone to lend a hand."

"I don't think that will be necessary. The fact is, it may take hours."

This, Maigret felt, was what he ought to have thought of doing at the outset. It had occurred to him, fleetingly, but then it had gone right out of his mind.

"Would you like me to send out for some beer? There's a bistro across the way. We often . . ."

"Thanks, but I've just had a glass."

As soon as he was alone he took off his jacket, rolled up his shirt sleeves, and went to the shelves to find the volume for the year 1945.

It took him an hour to work through it. Needless to say, he read only the headlines. None of them seemed to have any bearing on the lives of Marcel Vivien, Nina Lassave, or Louis Mahossier.

He returned the volume to its place on the shelves and,

oppressed by a slight headache, started on the year 1946. Twice the editor looked in to ask if there was anything he could do to help.

"Still not feeling thirsty?"

"I could do with a beer now, I have to admit."

The air was blue with smoke from his pipe. The room smelled of old paper and printer's ink.

Some of the headlines took him by surprise, recalling old scandals and sensational news items that were now completely forgotten.

January...February...March...April...

He plodded his way through to August, and there, in the issue for the seventeenth, he was confronted with the following headline:

YOUNG WOMAN FOUND STRANGLED

ON BOULEVARD ROCHECHOUART

The headline was not particularly prominent, nor was it on the front page. At the time, presumably, it had not attracted much attention.

A young woman, Nina Lassave, aged twenty-two, was found strangled in the bedroom of her apartment on Boulevard Rochechouart. She was lying naked on the bed. Nothing seemed to have been disturbed, either in the bedroom or elsewhere in the apartment. In reply to questioning, the concierge was unable to supply any significant information.

It was known that there was a man in her life, but he seldom visited her apartment. What precisely was it that occurred on the night of her death? The facts will be hard to establish. The concierge, as it happens, is an elderly woman, not much interested in the coming and goings of her tenants and their visitors.

The inquiry is being conducted by Chief Superintendent Piedboeuf of the Criminal Police.

The following day, under the headline NO NEW DEVELOPMENTS ON THE BOULEVARD ROCHECHOUART CASE, it was stated in a brief paragraph that nothing fresh had come to light regarding the young woman's private life. According to the police doctor's report, couched in technical language, the cause of death was strangulation. There were no signs of any other injuries on the body.

In response to further questioning, the concierge had confirmed that the girl had occasionally returned home in company with a youngish man, who usually went up with her to her apartment, though he had never once spent the night there.

The concierge had caught a glimpse of him once or twice. Nevertheless, she had thought it unlikely that she would recognize him again. During the last two months or so of her life the young woman had had another regular visitor, who used to visit her in the afternoon. The light being better at that time of day, the concierge had had a good look at him and was able to give a fuller description.

He was exceptionally tall and thin, with dark eyes. He always bounded up the stairs two at a time and left, unaccompanied, about an hour later.

There followed three blank days, before it was announced in the *Parisien Libéré* that:

A man has been at Police Headquarters helping Chief Superintendent Piedboeuf with his inquiries.

An atmosphere of great secrecy surrounds the interrogation of a suspect presently being held at Police Headquarters. The facts of the matter are that the tall, thin man, known to have visited Nina Lassave on several occasions in her apartment on Boulevard Rochechouart, has been identified as one Louis M., a house painter, who lives in a hotel in the vicinity.

He does not deny having been the lover of the young woman, but maintains that he did not see her on the day she died. The concierge, however, claims to have seen him on the stairs, on his way up, on that very day, at approximately four o'clock in the afternoon.

In the absence of any concrete evidence, the police have released M., but their inquiries continue.

As to Marcel V., cabinetmaker, who was Nina Lassave's

lover for at least six months before her death, there are wit-nesses to prove that he was seen in a café on Boulevard de la Chapelle at the time the murder was committed.

Maigret made notes in his old black notebook. The waiter from the local brasserie had brought him a glass of beer with a good head on it, and this, combined with the interest aroused by the newspaper revelations, had dispelled his headache.

He tried to find his way back to the editor's office, but got hopelessly lost in the maze of hallways and had to ask for directions.

"Would you mind if I had photostat copies made of one or two items from your archives?"

"Not in the least."

"May I use your phone?"

He asked to be put through to Moers.

"Is Mestral there . . . ? Send him over to the office of the *Parisien Libéré*, will you? Tell him to ask at the desk for the Archives Room. I'll be there, waiting for him."

Maigret returned to his researches among the old news-papers. As time went on, less and less space was devoted to Nina Lassave; a sensational political trial was getting under way, and that riveted the attention of readers all over France.

It now appears that Louis M., allegedly seen by the con-cierge going upstairs to Nina Lassave's apartment at about four o'clock on the afternoon of her death, also has an alibi. Chief Superintendent Piedboeuf and his team of inspectors are continuing their inquiries, but apparently have been un-able to discover any fresh evidence.

That more or less sounded the death knell in the stories about the Boulevard Rochechouart affair. There was no photograph of Mahossier or Marcel Vivien in any issue of the paper.

Mahossier had been summoned to the Quai des Orfèvres for questioning on two or three further occasions. The interrogations had been made under the auspices of Judge Coméliau, who was still alive at the time, but there had been no follow-up.

Half an hour later Mestral arrived, with a regular arsenal of cameras and flash-bulb equipment.

"How much is there to photograph?"

"Only about half a dozen shortish paragraphs."

Maigret watched him at work, indicating the relevant material as required.

"Could you manage to let me have some roughs by this afternoon?"

"They should be ready by four o'clock, unless it's so urgent that you'd rather I skipped lunch."

Maigret went in to thank the editor.

"Did you find what you wanted?"

"Yes."

"Presumably you want it kept under wraps for the time being?"

"When the time comes to release the story, I promise you'll be the first to know."

"Thanks. See you again very soon, I hope."

It was a few minutes past twelve. It was not much more than half an hour's walk from the Rue d'Enghien to Boulevard Richard-Lenoir. Maigret, in good spirits, enjoyed looking at the people, the tour buses, and the goods displayed in the shopwindows. Two or three buses were parked near Place de la Bastille, and cameras clicked as the tourists snapped it, to take its place alongside the Arc de Triomphe, the Sacré-Coeur, and the Tour Eiffel. Most of them looked a little weary, but all were determined to miss none of the sights they had been promised.

He was humming as he let himself into his apartment.

"Things are looking up, it seems," remarked Madame Maigret, as she served the hors d'oeuvres.

"I think I've done a good morning's work. I can't say yet what it may lead to, but it will lead to something, that's certain. There's one man, unfortunately, who will never come forward as a witness."

"Who is that?"

"Marcel Vivien. I've learned one thing, at any rate, and there's no reason for me to keep it secret. Nina Lassave was murdered, in her apartment, in August 1946."

"Was she shot?"

"No, strangled."

"No wonder you couldn't trace her."

"Exactly. And the more I question Mahossier, the more stubborn he gets."

He dug into his food with a will. They had a leg of lamb, which was pink and juicy, with the merest bead of blood forming on the bone.

"Delicious," he said with a sigh, and had another slice.

"Would you say the end was in sight?"

"I can't say anything definite at this stage, but I imagine we still have some way to go. The joke is that everything I found this morning in the back numbers of the *Parisien Libéré* must have been available from the first, only in greater detail, in the files of Criminal Records. The reason it slipped my mind was that it all happened during the time we were in Luçon."

"I was never so bored in my life!"

"You can say that again!"

"Would you like a peach? They're ripe and sweet."

"I won't say no."

He was at peace with himself and the world.

This time, returning to the Quai, he treated himself to a taxi. As on the previous day, the windows of his office were wide open, and little eddies of cooler air livened the room.

"Torrence!"

"Yes, Chief?"

"Have you finished typing that statement?"

"It's been ready since well before lunch."

"Let me have a copy, will you?"

When Torrence had brought it to him, he went on:

"I want you to go up to Records. Somewhere in the files for 1946 you're bound to find some material on the murder of Nina Lassave on Boulevard Rochechouart."

"That seems to ring a bell. . . . Ah! I remember now. . . . It was one of Chief Superintendent Piedboeuf's cases."

"Right. I want to see the file as soon as you can lay your hands on it."

Pausing occasionally for thought or to relight his pipe, he read carefully through the transcript of the questions and answers that he and Mahossier had exchanged that morning.

Every word was significant.

On paper, Mahossier's statement looked a lot more incoherent than it had sounded at the time.

When he had finished Maigret sat very still, with his eyes half-closed. Anyone watching might have thought he was asleep, but his mind was furiously active. He was endeavoring to recall every aspect of the inquiry, down to the smallest detail, to build up a coherent picture in his mind.

On a sudden impulse, he decided to telephone Ascan, the Superintendent of Police in the First Arrondissement.

"I'm terribly sorry, Chief Superintendent. I have no further progress to report."

"That's not why I called you. Could you possibly get hold of those two vagrants, the man and the woman, whom I spoke to in your office, and send them both to see me here. I'd be most grateful."

"I hope you don't catch their fleas!"

"It wouldn't be the first time. It's an occupational risk."

"We get more than our share of them in this district. What time do you want them to be there?"

"About four, if possible."

"We'll do our best. Some of my men here specialize in that sort of work."

Maigret asked the switchboard operator to put him through to Maître Loiseau in the Boulevard Beaumarchais. She called back almost at once to say that Loiseau was not at his office but could probably be found at the Palais de Justice.

"Try to get hold of him there."

This time Maigret was kept waiting for a quarter of an hour before his telephone rang again.

"Maître Loiseau speaking . . ."

"This is Chief Superintendent Maigret. Here is my story: In connection with a recent murder case, I brought a man in for questioning. His name is Louis Mahossier, and I understand that he's a client of yours. . . . This morning I tried to question him, but didn't get very far. He refuses to talk except in your presence. Well, I have no objection to that. . . . I wonder if you could possibly manage to be here, in my office, at about four?"

"I'm afraid I couldn't make it at four. . . . My case doesn't come up till three. Would five o'clock suit you?"

"Fine. I look forward to seeing you then."

Scarcely had Maigret replaced the receiver when Torrence came in with a slim file containing the documents relating to the murder of Nina Lassave in 1946. Having taken off his jacket and relighted his pipe, Maigret sat down at his desk to study it.

The first document was a signed statement made at the local police station by the concierge. Although the girl had come in early the previous night, she had not yet appeared downstairs by two o'clock the following afternoon, so the concierge had gone up to her room and knocked at the door.

Finding the door on the latch, she had gone into the apartment.

Everything seemed in order. The contents of the drawers had not been disturbed. The same was true of the bedroom, where she discovered the poor young woman lying, stark-naked, on the bed, with her tongue hanging out and her lifeless eyes turned up toward the ceiling.

Next followed a statement from the local Police Superintendent, whose name was Maillefer. He had visited the scene of the crime, accompanied by a Constable Patou. They had found the victim in the condition described by the concierge. Her clothes, among which was a print dress, were neatly folded on a chair not far from the bed.

"Robbery was plainly not the motive for the murder. Furthermore, in view of the victim's state of undress and the fact that she had made no attempt to cover herself up or fend him off, she must have been on terms of intimacy with the murderer. . . ."

The local Superintendent had called Chief Superintendent Piedboeuf who said he would come at once, reminding the officers that everything should be left exactly as they had found it and nothing touched. He also had asked them to inform the Public Prosecutor's Department.

If Maigret's memory served him right, Piedboeuf at the time must have been a little under fifty-five. He knew his job inside out and was not a man to be trifled with. If anything, he was rather too brusque and impatient.

He had been accompanied by two inspectors, one of whom still worked in the General Information Section.

Piedboeuf's report was fairly long, and attached to it was a floor plan of the apartment.

"None of the furniture seems to have been disturbed in any of the rooms, and I found three hundred francs in the victim's handbag, which was lying openly on the bedside table."

Attached to the Chief Superintendent's first report were two later ones, and also several photographs of Nina as she had been found. The first of the two reports was Moers's. He stated that his men had searched in vain for fingerprints. Apart from the victim's there were none, except for those of the concierge on the doorknobs.

Maigret was making notes.

The other report had the signature of Dr. Paul, with whom Maigret had worked for many years, but who was, regrettably, now dead. He had been Chief Forensic Officer and a great expert on food.

Translated from his technical language, his conclusion was that the victim had suffered death by strangulation. The marks of the murderer's fingers were clearly distinguishable on the girl's neck, and these indicated that the killer had unusually powerful hands.

The other tenants in the building had been questioned. There were not many of them. No one had heard anything. No one had seen any suspicious comings or goings on the stairs.

"Did Nina Lassave have many visitors?"

"No."

"But surely she had at least one fairly regular visitor?"

"There were two men who used to visit her."

"Together?"

"No. Separately. The taller one usually came sometime in midafternoon. . . . The other one would call for her in the evening. They used to go out together. I don't know where they usually went, but I did catch sight of them one day, or, rather, I should say one night, on the terrace of the Cyrano. . . ."

"Which of the two had she known longer?"

"The one who came in the evening. . . . The other one had only been coming for a couple of months or so. . . ."

"Did you see either of them on the stairs on the day of the murder?"

"To tell you the truth, I didn't set foot outside my apartment until after six."

The other tenants had even less to tell. One of them, an elderly bachelor, who worked in a bank on one of the Grands Boulevards, routinely left the house at eight in the morning and did not return until nine at night.

"I didn't even know the woman existed, let alone anything about the comings and goings of her men friends."

It was through the concierge that the police had got on Mahossier's track. He had turned up one day in a panel truck inscribed, in gold letters: LESAGE AND GÉLOT, PAINTING AND DECORATING, BOULEVARD DES BATIGNOLLES.

More reports and statements. Even the most trivial questions put to a witness were faithfully recorded in the usual stilted language. If he were to come across one of his own reports written at that period, Maigret wondered, would he find it equally quaint?

"As instructed by Chief Superintendent Piedboeuf, I

visited the premises of Messieurs Lesage and Gélot, painters and decorators, number twenty-five Boulevard des Batignolles. Monsieur Lesage was absent, but I obtained an interview with Monsieur Gélot. I inquired of him how many workmen he employed, to which he replied that, this being the slack season, he had at present only four men on his books.

"He supplied me with their names. I asked him their ages. Three of them were over forty, one, in fact, being a man of sixty.

"Only one, a man of the name of Louis Mahossier, was young, aged twenty-six. I had to wait for nearly half an hour, because Mahossier was out delivering materials to a building site. He was driving the truck described by the concierge at Boulevard Rochechouart.

"Mahossier took it very much amiss. He demanded to know by what right I was subjecting him to such questioning and at first denied ever having met Nina Lassave. I asked him to accompany me to Boulevard Rochechouart. The concierge remembered him very well. He was undoubtedly the man she had met on the stairs two days previously, at about the time the young woman was killed.

"In view of this, I asked him to accompany me to the Quai des Orfèvres, where I handed him over to my superior officer, Chief Superintendent Piedboeuf."

Maigret mopped his face.

Mahossier had been questioned on four separate occasions, and he had stuck to his original story throughout. On the day in question, he claimed, at about the time when the murder was taking place, he had been in one of the firm's trucks, delivering drums of paint to an address on Rue de Courcelles.

The fellow workmen who had taken delivery of the paint had confirmed his story, but had been much more vague about the time of delivery.

Coméliau, the Examining Magistrate on the case, had sent for him and questioned him in his turn.

Other witnesses questioned had included Marcel Vivien

as well as the proprietor and a waiter from the café on
Boulevard de la Chapelle.

Vivien had appeared stunned. The death of his mistress
seemed to have left him drained of all energy. Since there
was no evidence against him, he had been allowed to return to his room on Place des Abbesses.

The authorities had persisted longer with Mahossier, but
in the end, having too little to go on, they had decided to
leave him in peace.

The file was not actually marked "Case Closed," because
the police never formally close an unsolved murder case,
but in practice it came to the same thing.

"Torrence! Be a good fellow and bring Mahossier here
from the cells in about a quarter of an hour."

As for himself, he intended to slip out to the Brasserie
Dauphine for a quick beer. If Maître Loiseau proved to be
as stubborn as his client, the forthcoming session was going
to be no picnic.

When he got back Mahossier was already installed in a
chair in his office, and Inspector Torrence had his shorthand notebook open on the desk.

"We can't start without Maître Loiseau."

Mahossier pretended not to have heard. Maigret idly
turned over the pages of the file, committing to memory
one or two final details.

Maître Loiseau arrived, still in his robes, having come
straight from the Palais de Justice by way of the connecting
entrance to Police Headquarters.

"I'm terribly sorry, but my case started a quarter of an
hour late. . . ."

"Do please sit down. I have a number of questions to put
to your client. Up to now, he has persisted in denying
everything. I take it you know what the charge is?"

"The charge! Aren't you getting a bit ahead of yourself?
As I understand it, the interrogation hasn't even started."

"Very well, let's put it another way. Your client is suspected of the murder of a vagrant, Marcel Vivien, in a
condemned building in Vieux-Four Passage."

Maigret turned to Mahossier.

"To begin with, I can prove that you were in the district on the night in question."

"Are your witnesses reliable?"

"You may judge for yourself."

He sent Torrence out to fetch the man known as Toto, who had been brought to Headquarters, along with the bloated Nana, by an inspector from the First Arrondissement. Toto, who felt quite at home with the police, was not in the least overawed. He looked boldly from one to another of those present. When his glance fell on Mahossier, his face lighted up.

"Well! Fancy seeing you, pal! How are you, old friend? I hope you're not in any trouble."

"So you know this man?" Maigret asked. "Can you tell me exactly where and when you met him?"

"In Les Halles, of course. Where else? I spend every night of my life there. . . ."

"Can you tell us exactly where you were at the time . . . ?"

"Not ten yards away from Chez Pharamond . . . I was watching a truck being unloaded. One of my buddies was working on it . . . if you could call him a buddy, because, to be frank, he wasn't really buddies with anyone. . . . His name was Vivien. He was unloading vegetables, and I was waiting for another truck to turn up so that I could get myself taken on."

"What happened next?"

"The door of Chez Pharamond opened, and this gentleman came out of the restaurant. He stood there for quite a while watching the fellows unloading. I made the most of it by going up to him and asking him to let me have the price of a glass of red wine. Instead of giving me a franc, as I expected, he gave me a five-franc piece, enough to buy myself a whole bottle."

"Had you ever seen him at Les Halles before?"

"Never."

"Do you go there often?"

"I told you, I've been going every night for the past fifteen years."

"You are at liberty to question this witness if you wish, Maître."

"The night you were telling us about, what date was that?"

"As if I keep account of dates! I can tell you one thing, at any rate. It was the night Vivien was done in."

"Are you sure?"

"Yes."

"Were you drunk, by any chance?"

"Sure I was, by three o'clock in the morning, but not at ten o'clock at night."

"Are you quite certain that this is the same man?"

"As sure as I am that he recognizes me. Just take a look at his face. . . ."

Maigret turned to Mahossier.

"Is that true?"

"I've never set eyes on the old rag bag before."

"Rag bag! Rag bag, did you say?"

Torrence propelled him protesting from the room, and ushered in the fat woman with the swollen legs and the fingers like sausages. Though somewhat unsteady on her feet, she was not yet completely drunk.

After sitting down, she looked about her and then raised her right hand and pointed to Mahossier.

"That's him," she said, sounding very hoarse, as no doubt she always did.

"What are you talking about?"

"I mean he's the man I saw coming out of that place where the dudes go for their grub—about ten o'clock at night, it was."

"Do you know the name of the restaurant?"

"Chez Pharamond."

"Are you sure this is the same man?"

"Positive. And I'm just as sure I saw Toto talking to him. He told me afterward that this same fellow had given him a five-franc piece, and he even went so far as to buy me a drink on the strength of it."

"Do you recognize her, Mahossier?"

"Certainly not. I've never seen the woman in my life, and she certainly never saw me in Les Halles."

Maigret turned to Nana.

"Did you see him again?"

"That same night, at about three in the morning. I was huddled in a doorway on the corner of the de la Grande-Truanderie and Vieux-Four Passage. I heard footsteps, and then someone brushed past me. A very tall, thin man he was. I knew him at once. You couldn't mistake him, especially since there is a street light just at the entrance to the passage."

"Did you see where he went?"

"Into one of those tumble-down houses that have been under a demolition order for the last ten years. I'm surprised they haven't collapsed already. . . ."

"Mahossier, do you or do you not recognize this woman?"

"I've never seen her. . . ."

Maître Loiseau remarked, with a sigh:

"Is this the best you can produce in the way of witnesses . . . ?"

"Take her outside, Torrence, will you."

"Shall I bring in the next witness?"

"In a minute . . . The first time I put the question to you, you denied having dined at Chez Pharamond on the night in question. Do you still deny it?"

"I most certainly do."

"In that case, where did you dine? Not at home, according to your own admission, because your mother-in-law was expected to dinner, and you and she are not on the best of terms."

"I went to a snack bar on one of the Grands Boulevards."

"Could you find it again?"

"I think so."

"Did you have anything to drink?"

"I don't drink, except for a glass of wine with my meals."

"In other words, you're saying you never set foot in Chez Pharamond?"

At a sign from Maigret, Torrence went out and returned with a man in his early fifties, completely dressed in black.

"Please be seated, Monsieur Genlis."

"In my professional capacity, I am generally known as Robert."

"Tell us about that. What is your profession, and where do you work?"

"I am assistant headwaiter at Chez Pharamond."

"And in that capacity, I presume, you pay particular attention to the arrival and departure of your patrons?"

"It's mostly my job to show them to their tables."

"Is there anyone in this room whose face is familiar to you?"

"Yes."

And he pointed to Mahossier, who this time turned a little pale.

"When did you last see him?"

"I only saw him once. That was last Monday evening. He was alone, which is fairly unusual for our patrons. He ate his meal rather fast, and then I showed him to the door and let him out."

"What do you say to that, Monsieur Mahossier?"

"It's ten years or more since I last set foot in Chez Pharamond. According to this man's own statement, he only saw me once, in a room crowded with people."

"How do you know it was crowded?"

"I presume it was, considering what a well-known place it is. . . ."

"I should point out," remarked the assistant headwaiter, "that one seldom sees a man so tall and thin."

"Any questions, Maître Loiseau?"

"None. My client reserves his defense for his official interrogation before an examining magistrate."

"Thank you, Monsieur Genlis. I needn't trouble you any further."

"Have you any other witnesses, Chief Superintendent?"

"As far as this particular matter is concerned, that's as far as we need go for today."

The lawyer, looking somewhat relieved, stood up.

"But there is still another matter to be considered."

"Another matter? Isn't it enough that you have accused my client of murdering a tramp whom he has never set eyes on?"

Mahossier himself now turned very pale indeed, and this accentuated the dark circles under his eyes and the harsh lines at the corners of his tight-lipped mouth.

"Please go on."

"Do you by any chance recall the sixteenth of August, 1946, Mahossier?"

"Certainly not. What reason could I possibly have for doing so? It must have been a working day like any other, because in those days I was saving every penny I could earn, and I couldn't afford vacations."

"You were an employee with the firm of Lesage and Gélot?"

"That is correct."

He seemed taken aback and a little uneasy.

"You frequently drove a panel truck bearing the name of the firm on the side?"

"Quite often, yes."

"On that day, you delivered a number of drums of paint to your fellow workers at a site on Rue de Courcelles."

"I can't remember."

"I have here a statement that you made to Chief Superintendent Piedboeuf. I presume you won't attempt to deny that you answered questions put to you by the Chief Superintendent on a number of occasions?"

Maigret passed the open file to him across the desk.

"What are you getting at?"

"Where were you living at the time?"

"I can't remember. I lived in hotels, and I never stayed anywhere for very long."

"Allow me to refresh your memory. You lived at the

Hôtel Jonard, on Place des Abbesses. Do you know who else lived in that hotel?"

"I didn't know any of the other tenants."

"You saw him again very recently, in Les Halles, for the first time in twenty years. I am referring to Marcel Vivien, who was, at that time, Nina Lassave's lover."

"That's no concern of mine."

"Oh, yes, it is, indeed. She visited Vivien frequently. I don't know whether you followed her home or what, but the fact remains that the concierge of the building where she lived recognized you as a man who came to see her regularly during the last two months of her life."

Maître Loiseau asked:

"Is the concierge here?"

"She died some time ago, after returning, on her retirement, to the village where she was born. . . ."

"In other words, you can't call her as a witness, which I assume suits your purposes very well. So far, all you have been able to produce is a couple of squalid, sottish drunks and a man who makes a living on tips, and now we are asked to take the word of a dead woman. What next, I wonder?"

"All in good time," murmured Maigret, refilling his pipe.

1 2 3 4

THE LAWYER CONSULTED HIS WATCH, WHICH
undoubtedly showed that it was ten past six, as did Maigret's.
He was still young and given to affecting an air of importance.
Brusquely he stood up.

"Have you finished with my client, Chief Superintendent?"

"I'm not sure."

"I'm afraid I shall have to go. I have an appointment
at my office in twenty minutes, and I mustn't be late."

The Chief Superintendent shrugged, as if to say:

"That's no concern of mine."

Loiseau turned to Mahossier.

"Let me give you a word of advice. If you are asked any
more questions, don't answer. That is your right under the
law. No one can compel you to say anything."

Mahossier did not respond. His manner was more sober,
less aggressive. He was beginning to appreciate the gravity
of the situation, it seemed, and also to realize that the
lawyer's chief concern was his own self-importance.

Maître Loiseau bustled out, looking as pompous as when
he had come in. Maigret murmured, as if in passing:

"Let me give you a word of advice. If you are committed
for trial at the Assizes, change your lawyer. That fellow will
only antagonize the court."

He went on:

"He's quite right in saying that you cannot be compelled

to answer questions, but, in the eyes of many, silence is taken to indicate guilt, if not to prove it. I'm not going to ask you any further questions, but I would be obliged if you would listen to what I have to say, and please feel free to interrupt if there is any comment you wish to make."

He was watching Mahossier closely. It seemed to him that the man's manner had become less aggressive than it was in La Baule or when he was first brought in for questioning. Now, his expression was more that of an overgrown school-boy who is keeping up a pretense of sulking even when he no longer feels like it.

"Chief Superintendent Piedboeuf was an excellent police officer, and by no means the sort to resent being proved wrong. Is it not a fact that Nina Lassave had a strawberry birthmark on her left cheek?"

"Is this a trap?"

"Nothing so subtle. There is evidence enough here in this file to prove that you were indeed this woman's lover."

"The concierge is dead."

"That doesn't invalidate her testimony. Here, for instance, is the transcript of an exchange between the two of you when you were brought face to face:

"You asked her, somewhat aggressively:

" 'How did you know my name?'

"Apparently you thought she would be hard put to find an answer to that. This, however, is her reply:

" 'I was in my lodge one afternoon, having tea with a friend who calls to see me from time to time. I can give you her name and address if you wish. As we were sitting there, this man'—pointing to you—'came in through the archway, and we got a clear view of him through the glass door. My friend started in surprise.

" ' "Well! Well!" she said. "If it isn't my painter! He's the one who painted my kitchen and laid the carpet in the dining room. His name is Louis Mahossier, and he works for a firm on Boulevard des Batignolles." ' "

"This friend of the concierge, whose name was Lucile Gosset, was interviewed, and she confirmed what she had previously said. It was as a direct result of this that you were traced so soon.

"On the day Nina was killed, at about four o'clock in the afternoon, you were working in the widow Gosset's apartment on Rue Ballu. At about that time she went out to do her shopping, and you at once seized the opportunity of driving straight to Rue Rochechouart. . . ."

Mahossier was watching him, frowning. He seemed puzzled, as though searching for some explanation that continued to elude him.

"I can, if you wish, read you the concierge's statement. The mailman called with a special-delivery letter for one of the tenants on the third floor, and the concierge took it up to her. As she was coming downstairs again she passed you on the way up to Nina's apartment. Do you still persist in denying all this?"

There was no answer. As he listened to Maigret, Louis Mahossier seemed to grow calmer, though it was clear that he was still under considerable strain.

"You were both crazy about her. I don't know what it was about her that aroused such intense feelings. Marcel Vivien abandoned his wife and child for her. And yet she wouldn't even go and live with him. She never spent a single night in his company. Nor in yours, for that matter. I don't know whether it was just some lingering inhibition due to her upbringing. . . ."

Maigret's voice was muted. From time to time, mechanically, he riffled through the pages of the file that lay open in front of him.

"To get back to the afternoon of Nina's murder, undeniably Marcel Vivien had an alibi, but it was by no means watertight."

Mahossier was now watching the Chief Superintendent more intently.

"This morning I came across a note written in the margin of the file by my predecessor, Piedboeuf. It reads as follows:

" 'Received an unsolicited visit from an old man, a regular of the bistro on Boulevard de la Chapelle, named Arthur

Gilson, nicknamed Peg Leg because he has a stiff knee joint and walks as if he had a wooden leg. He had obviously been drinking.

" 'He claims that on the afternoon in question Marcel Vivien came into the bistro at about half past three and tossed off two brandies, one after the other. He was very much struck by this because normally the cabinetmaker drank nothing but coffee. According to him, Vivien then made off in the direction of Boulevard Rochechouart.' "

Maigret looked up, and there was a moment's silence as he gazed searchingly at Mahossier.

"It is only fair to tell you that of all the other people who were in the bistro at the time, not one was able to confirm his story. Or, rather, the proprietor did confirm that the events as described took place, but on the day after Nina's death.

"One of the two witnesses must have been right and the other wrong. My predecessor seems to have favored the proprietor's version."

Mahossier could not resist asking:

"And you?"

"I'm inclined to believe Peg Leg. He was old, but perfectly coherent. He is now dead. All we have to go on is this marginal note by Chief Superintendent Piedboeuf. . . . Nina had been Vivien's mistress for more than six months. Having severed all ties with his family, he looked upon her as his exclusive property. . . . Then she met you, and even after her relations with you she still maintained her intimacy with Vivien.

"Vivien seldom visited her in the afternoon. They had formed the habit of lunching together in a restaurant and meeting again in the evening."

Once more Mahossier's expression hardened.

"At the time of the inquiry, the concierge could not recall having seen him arrive or leave. Asked what she had been doing at the time, she replied that she had been sitting by the window, knitting and listening to the radio. Now, from that part of the room, she need not have noticed everyone coming in and going out through the archway."

"What are you getting at?"

"I am suggesting that it was Vivien who killed his mistress, who was also your mistress. It's possible that he actually saw you leave the building. We will never know. One thing we can be sure of is that he was beside himself, literally torn apart by grief.

"It's unlikely that he went to Boulevard Rochechouart with the intention of killing her, and he was certainly unarmed. It may be that all he had in mind was to surprise you together.

"He found her lying naked on the bed. Why should she have taken off her clothes unless she was expecting a lover?

"He felt that he had done everything for her sake. Had he not shamefully abandoned his wife and daughter, leaving them without a penny? And now, here she was, deceiving him with the first man who came along.

"I don't know what they said to each other. But one thing is clear. Nina Lassave was unable to quiet him down. She was not frightened—witness the way she was lying when they found her. . . . But he was working himself up into a state of frenzy, driving himself to such a pitch that he ended up by strangling her. He could see his whole life crumbling in ruins. . . . He could never again return to the Rue Caulaincourt, still less to his workshop on Rue Lepic. Nothing mattered to him any more. Though it might have given him some satisfaction if they had succeeded in pinning the murder on you. . . ."

"It's what they tried to do, more or less, and you, too, at the beginning. I always said I hadn't killed her."

"When did you find out that she was dead?"

"A quarter of an hour later. I saw Vivien hurry out of the building. He almost ran as far as Place Blanche. I suddenly felt I had to go up and ask Nina what he had come for.

"I went inside, and it was then that I bumped into the concierge on the stairs. When I got to the apartment the door was on the latch. That struck me as odd. A couple of minutes later, I found the body. . . . That was when I removed all the fingerprints. I wiped everything I had ever touched, not only then, but on earlier occasions. That meant I also had to get rid of Vivien's fingerprints. . . ."

"Why didn't you report him to the police?"

"Because I'd made up my mind to deal with him myself. . . ."

Poor Torrence was having difficulty keeping up with the rapid tempo of his speech. There was no more question of a monologue delivered by Maigret. A genuine dialogue was developing.

Maigret had penetrated Mahossier's defenses, and he was cracking up.

"You really loved her that much?"

"She's the only woman I have ever truly loved."

"What about the woman you married?"

"I'm very fond of her, and she is of me, I believe. But it was never an overwhelming passion for either of us."

"Twenty years have gone by, Mahossier."

"I know. All the same, there isn't a day passes that I don't think of her."

"Don't you realize that the same was true of Vivien? He loved her every bit as passionately as you did, passionately enough to kill her. He never tried to make a new life for himself, but chose, rather, to spend the rest of his days in the lowest depths. He became a derelict, and so remained, until you saw him again quite by chance after twenty years."

1 2 3 4

IN SILENCE, MAHOSSIER GAZED FIXEDLY DOWN AT HIS shoes. His face had undergone a change. He looked much less arrogant and, in consequence, much more human.

"You have had twenty good years. . . ."

He looked up at Maigret, his thin lips twisted into a half-smile expressing his awareness of the irony of the situation.

"I didn't kill her, it's true. And yet it is no less true that indirectly I was the cause of her death. . . ."

"You worked hard, and you saved. You managed to set up in business on your own, and things went well for you. You have a charming and attractive wife, a magnificent apartment, and a villa in La Baule. . . . And yet you were prepared to risk losing all that you had built up, to kill a man whom you hadn't seen for twenty years and who, in the meantime, had degenerated into a wreck. . . ."

"I had sworn an oath that I would punish him."

"Could you not have left that to the law?"

"He would have claimed that it was a *crime passionnel* and gotten off with a light sentence. By this time he would have been a free man for many years. . . ."

"Your lawyer will claim on your behalf that the killing of Vivien was also a *crime passionnel*. . . ."

"I don't care any more. Only yesterday I was determined to deny everything . . . to defend myself. . . .

"The fact is that, whatever you may think, the burden is too heavy for me."

The telephone rang.

"Ascan speaking, First Arrondissement. All going well?"

"Fine. I've had Mahossier here with me in my office for the last two hours."

"Has he confessed?"

"Yes."

"He would have had to anyway, however reluctantly. Some kids who were playing on a vacant lot near the derelict house where Vivien shacked up have just handed me a thirty-two pistol. Three bullets are missing from the magazine. One of my men is on the way to the Quai now, to hand it over to you personally."

"It will be very useful as corroborative evidence."

"Did he kill Nina Lassave, too?"

"No."

"Who did, then? Vivien?"

"Yes."

"Do you mean to say that Mahossier was still so much in love with Nina Lassave, after twenty years, that he was prepared to kill to avenge her murder?"

"Yes . . . Thank you very much, Ascan. You've been a tremendous help to me. . . . In fact, you and your men have done most of the work in this case."

"Oh, I wouldn't say that! . . . Anyway, I mustn't keep you from your work any longer."

Mahossier had been doing his best to follow the conversation, but he could hear only Maigret's side of it, which gave away very little.

"So you spent the last twenty years searching Paris for him?"

"I wouldn't go as far as that. . . . I did look at the faces of people in the streets. I was convinced, I don't know why, that someday I would see him again. You were right in saying that I dined at Chez Pharamond that night. I walked from my apartment to Les Halles. It brought back old memories. In the old days, I had looked on Chez Pharamond as the height of luxury, a mecca of self-indulgence far beyond my means. I went in, was shown to a table, and dined alone. My mother-in-law can't stand me, and she's always making snide remarks. She can't forgive me for having started out as a house painter. . . . Besides, she somehow found out that I was born in Belleville and that I was illegitimate."

A few minutes later old Joseph, the messenger, knocked at the door.

"There's an inspector here from the First Arrondissement. He has a parcel, which he says he has instructions to hand to you personally."

"Send him in."

The inspector turned out to be young and very eager.

"I came as soon as I could, Chief Superintendent. I have instructions to give you this."

He held out a parcel wrapped in dirty wrinkled brown paper. He looked at Mahossier with frank curiosity.

"Do you wish me to stay?"

"That won't be necessary. Thank you."

As soon as the inspector had gone Maigret opened the package.

"This is your gun, isn't it?"

"It looks like it, at any rate."

"So you see, even without your confession we would have arrived at the truth. Of course, we will have to check that the bullets in the gun match those removed from Vivien's chest. . . . You were so scared of being caught with this gun in your pocket that you got rid of it by dropping it on the first empty lot you came to. . . ."

Mahossier shrugged.

"It's quite true that I gave a five-franc piece to a tramp. I also saw the fat woman, who seemed to be dead drunk. When I recognized Vivien, unloading crates of vegetables, all the old rage boiled up in me again, and I rushed home to get my pistol. . . .

"I waited there in the dark street. . . . I had to wait a long time, because another truck had arrived and he was taken on, along with others, to unload it."

"And all this time your hatred remained at white heat?"

"No. I just felt I had a duty to accomplish."

"A duty to Nina?"

"Yes. But there was something else, as well. This man, this fellow Vivien, seemed at peace with himself. After all, he had chosen his way of life for himself, hadn't he? And through it, he seemed somehow to have found peace. I was infuriated. . . ."

"And, in this frame of mind, you hung around until three in the morning?"

"Not quite that long . . . Till about half past two. . . . Then I followed him as far as Vieux-Four Passage. The fat woman I had seen in Les Halles was crouching in a doorway. I thought she was asleep or in a drunken stupor. I never dreamed that she could be dangerous. Maître Loiseau will be furious with me for telling you all this, but nothing matters any more to me.

"I watched Vivien go into the house. . . . Shortly after, I followed him in and began creeping upstairs. I heard him shut his door. . . . I waited on the stairs for nearly half an hour. . . ."

"Were you waiting for him to fall asleep?"

"No. It was just that I couldn't make up my mind."

"What decided you in the end?"

"It was the thought of Nina, or, more precisely, the little strawberry mark on her cheek. It gave her such a fragile look, somehow. . . ."

"Did you find him awake?"

"After the first shot he opened his eyes. He looked surprised. I can't say whether he recognized me. . . ."

"Didn't you speak to him?"

"No. Maybe I was sorry I'd come, but it was too late by then. The only reason I fired the other two shots was to spare him pain. Believe it or not, as you please."

"And yet you tried to get away with it?"

"That's true. I suppose it was more instinctive than anything else. Vivien also had failed to give himself up, after he killed the woman he loved. . . ."

A spasm of anguish passed over his face as he spoke those last words. Then once more he shrugged.

"By the way, what became of Madame Vivien?"

"She's still alive, living in a smaller apartment in the same building on Rue Caulaincourt. She's become a dressmaker. She seems to have built up quite a nice little business."

"There was a daughter, too, wasn't there?"

"She's married and has two children."

"I hope all this hasn't been too painful for them."

On this point Maigret preferred to say nothing.

"What are you going to do with me?"

"For the present, you will return to your cell. Tomorrow you will be formally interrogated by the Examining Magistrate, who will probably sign a warrant for your arrest. Until that stage of the proceedings is completed, you will probably be detained in the Santé. Later, I expect you will be moved to Fresnes prison, where you will remain until your trial."

"Won't I be allowed to see my wife?"

"Not for the first few days, I'm afraid."

"When will the news of my arrest be in the papers?"

"Tomorrow. I believe a reporter is already waiting outside with a photographer."

Maigret felt a little weary. He, too, had been suddenly relieved of a heavy burden, and it had left him feeling hollow inside. His voice sounded strained. Certainly he felt easier in his mind, but he did not feel triumphant.

Searching for one murderer, he had found two. Was that the solution he had been groping toward all along?

"I am going to ask you a favor, which I suppose you won't be able to grant me. I would like to spare my wife the distress of learning about my arrest from the newspapers or, worse, through a phone call from her mother or a friend. She should be in the middle of dinner by now. At any rate, I'm sure she's back at the villa."

"What is her telephone number?"

"La Baule one two four."

"Hello! Miss, would you please get me La Baule one two four. Yes, it is urgent. . . ."

It was he, rather than the accused man, who was longing to be free. Within three minutes the call went through.

"Is that the 'Umbrella Pines'?"

"Yes."

"Madame Mahossier? This is Maigret speaking. Your husband is here with me in my office. He would like a word with you."

Maigret stumped over to the window and stood there, puffing furiously at his pipe.

"Yes. I'm at Police Headquarters. Are you alone?"

"Except for the maid."

"Listen carefully. . . . You're in for a severe shock. . . ."

"Do you think so?"

"Yes . . . I have just confessed to the murder of Marcel Vivien."

Contrary to his expectation, she took it calmly.

"Because of a woman?"

"What do you mean?"

"What else could it be?"

"He killed her . . . twenty years ago . . . I knew that it was Vivien, but he disappeared. . . ."

"I had a feeling . . . And when you saw him again, after twenty years, all the old jealousy built up again. . . ."

"You guessed?"

"I suspected it from the first."

"How could you?"

"Because I know you. . . ."

"What will you do?"

"To begin with, I'll stay on here, unless the Examining Magistrate wants me in Paris. After that, I'm not sure yet.

There's never been any great love between us, after all. . . .
The fact is, I was never anything more than a substitute.
. . . I guess my mother will nag me into divorcing you. . . ."

"Oh!"

"Does that surprise you?"

"No . . . I suppose not. . . . Good-by, Margot. . . ."

"Good-by, Louis."

As he hung up the receiver he swayed and almost fell.
He had not expected things to turn out quite like this.
It was not so much what had been said as all that it
had implied. More than ten years of his life had been wiped
out by a conversation lasting a few minutes.

Maigret went to his cupboard and poured a little brandy
into a glass.

"Here, drink this."

Mahossier, hesitating, looked at Maigret in amazement.

"I had no idea . . ." he stammered.

"No idea that your wife had guessed the truth?"

"She's going to divorce me."

"What else did you expect? That she would wait for
you?"

"I no longer know what to think."

He gulped down his brandy and coughed. Then, making
no attempt to sit down again, he murmured:

"It was good of you not to harass me. . . ."

"Take him back to the cells, Torrence."

Fat Torrence looked upset. Mahossier stood waiting for
him in the middle of the room. In a curious way, he appeared to have shrunk, and in his bewilderment he suddenly
seemed insignificant.

He started to hold out his hand, but then changed his
mind.

"Good-by, Chief Superintendent."

"Good-by."

Maigret felt drowsy. Heavily he paced the room while
awaiting Torrence's return.

"Do you know?" Torrence remarked, when he got back.

"At one point, I really felt quite moved."

"What about coming with me to the Brasserie Dauphine for a glass of something?"

"I'd be glad to."

They walked side by side from the Quai des Orfèvres to the bar they knew so well. There were several inspectors already in the bar, but only one from the Crime Squad.

"What's yours, Chief Superintendent?" asked the proprietor.

"A long beer. In the tallest glass you've got."

Torrence ordered the same. Maigret drank his down almost in one gulp and held out the glass for a refill.

"It's thirsty weather today. . . ."

Maigret repeated the words mechanically, as though they had no meaning for him:

"Thirsty weather, yes."

He went home in a taxi.

"I was wondering whether you'd be home in time for dinner."

He flopped into his armchair and mopped his face.

"As far as my part in the business is concerned, the case is over."

"Has the killer been arrested?"

"Yes."

"The man you went to see in La Baule?"

"Yes."

"How about going out to eat? All I've got here is some cold meat and Russian salad."

"I'm not hungry."

"It's all on the table. You might as well have it."

That evening he felt no inclination to look at television, and by ten o'clock he was in bed.